CW00498032

WOMEN ARE BLOODY MARVELLOUS!

AND OTHER STORIES

WOMEN ARE BLOODY MARVELLOUS!

AND OTHER STORIES

Betty Burton

GRAFTON BOOKS
A Division of the Collins Publishing Group

LONDON GLASGOW
TORONTO SYDNEY AUCKLAND

Grafton Books
A Division of the Collins Publishing Group
8 Grafton Street, London W1X 3LA

Published by Grafton Books 1986

Copyright © Betty Burton 1986

British Library Cataloguing in Publication Data
Burton, Betty
Women are bloody marvellous!
I. Title
823'.914[F] PR6052.U67/
ISBN 0-246-12800-3

Typeset by Columns of Reading
Printed in Great Britain by
Billings of Worcester

All rights reserved. No part of this publication may be reproduced, stored in a retrieval system, or transmitted, in any form or by any means, electronic, mechanical, photocopying, recording or otherwise, without the prior permission of the publisher.

CONTENTS

PULASKI DAY

PULASKI DAY

'If men and women are in chains anywhere in the world, then freedom is endangered.'

John F. Kennedy,
Pulaski Day, October 1969

1 THE ICE BEAR

South Africa is an unlikely place to see a polar bear for the first time, and that February it was ninety in the shade.

We had been living in Johannesburg for about a year, had experienced the freeze-drying winds of June and Christmas in mid-summer.

We were still strangers.

I had not wanted to go there, not even for three years, but John had a contract with IBCC and I had a contract with John. Nobody lightly broke an IBCC contract and the one between me and John was for better or worse.

Many people wouldn't have wanted asking twice – three years in a beautiful country, where summers were hot and long and where you could get servants for next to nothing. We were given a company car, and a flat in the airy suburbs paid for by IBCC, the rent of which included burglar-proofing, cooker, fridge and Sara. That's just how IBCC arranged things there – a company man was given a chauffeur and secretary, a company wife was expected to have a maid.

It was an absurd set-up: the flat was full of labour-saving devices and all the cleaning was done by a gang of African men who spent their days on their knees or up ladders so that Sara and I had only my two small boys to look after between us. So we spent a lot of time doing what Sara loved to do, 'going somewhere out'.

There was no garden to the flat, but there were 'Residents Only' grounds, the lawned dignity of which made boys aged three and seven with a ball appear as hooligans. So at about mid-day, when school had ended, Sara and I often took them to the zoo.

We lived about fifteen minutes' walk away so, as soon as we had finished our brief lunch, we would take the lift down from the cool flat and go out into the hard-hitting African sun. We would amble along until Sara gave us our orders.

'Stop. Here we play five-stones.' And she would make us squat under a jacaranda tree until she considered we had rested. Then a bit further.

'We shall get Coca-Cola you think, M'em?'

It didn't really much matter what M'em thought. Sara made up the rules, we played her game.

Eventually we got to the zoo, and inside, as on the walk, we kept to a daily routine following the same paths, stopping at the same places. I don't know why we did it, it is such a huge park that we could have taken a different direction each time. Perhaps it was because there was something reassuring in knowing that around this bend would be the elephant house, around the next the lake, and over there was the café – all tangible, static, ordered. Perhaps these were the new corner-stones of our lives, replacing the ones we had left in Ascot.

At some of the enclosures we lingered, visiting an interesting animal; others warranted only a few minutes or a passing glance, but the chipmunks were special – Simon, Brendan and Sara never tired of their greedy antics, and the caged tree was the focal point of the outing. I couldn't stand the creatures, perhaps I saw something in the look-after-number-one type of society that was too near home for comfort, so I went off for walks on my own.

I really liked that place. I have a passion for gardening which was excited by the exotic trees and flowers, and my anxieties and tangled nerves unwound beside the lake that reflected clear blue. There was a feeling there that I found nowhere else in South Africa. The whole area was surrounded by high fences and walls, and whenever I walked through the gates I felt that I was entering a kind of no-man's-land, buffer-zone, limbo perhaps, at any rate in the zoo park I could foster the illusion that it was just like home, that I was not living in the Republic.

Of course it was not just like home. 'NIE-BLANKE – NON-WHITES', 'WHITES ONLY', 'NO INSIDE SERVICE FOR NON-WHITES'. But at least in the zoo park the orders and notice-boards were faded, warped and peeling, giving the impression that whoever was in charge saw *homo sapiens* as merely another species of animal and was not much concerned with classifying it by its hide.

On that afternoon in February, I went in a direction that I didn't remember ever having taken before, and came to a railed-off area overlooking a concrete pit. In the pit was a small iron cage. I looked down, casually wondering whether there was something that the children had not seen before.

That was the first time I saw the bear.

The cage was small, and the bear enormous. There was room for him to take only three steps. I watched him pace back and forth, back and forth, back and forth in quick succession. It was nothing like the usual kind of prowling of large animals kept in cages, he just went on and on – fast – without pause. Not many people were looking at him, just a few zoo cleaners resting with chins on brushes, a middle-aged white couple in shorts and knee-socks, and a grey-haired African with a pattern of tribal scars on his cheeks, carrying a staff carved of wood.

The cleaners and the couple soon moved on, leaving me and the old man. He stood with his feet planted slightly apart, the carved staff in his right hand, back erect in the stance of a guardsman on duty outside Buckingham Palace, and for an instant I saw a glimpse of his ancestors, plumed and confident – before the white man came.

Watching animals in captivity is not something I like to do. When I took the kids to the zoo park I had a feeling that we weren't really living here at all. Yet I stood watching for a long time.

I had never seen a polar bear and I wanted to look closely. His massive volume was impressive, yet how light his steps were. I wished that he would be still, and stop the fast-moving blur as he paced and re-paced the cage. I wanted him to lie down and stretch out like a leopard so that I could really look at his form, could see why his fur appeared to be yellow instead of the expected white, look at the eyes and ears. But he moved and moved, fluffing the long hair of his coat.

'M'em?'

I was brought back from my absorbing attention to the bear. It was the African, standing at a respectful distance, who had spoken. His voice was rich and deep, and he inclined his head to one side as I noticed many older servants do when they ask a question of a 'Madam' or 'Baas'. I had seen plenty of such servants who had been with one family for a lifetime, taught early in life to know their place yet who, in spite of handed-down clothes, retained impressive dignity.

'Excuse me, M'em. Those zoo boys – they say this is the Ice Bear?'

'Yes, that's right. It's called a polar bear.'

'Is it true also that it lives at a place of only ice?'

'Yes, the land's covered most of the time.' I wondered if he could imagine such a place. It was likely that his only experience of ice was that which tinkled in the glasses he served.

He shook his head. 'That must be very strange to see. And cold.'

'Colder even than Jeppe Street when the wind blows.' It was a joke and he smiled. Soon I was again lost in watching the bear. There was something wrong. Suddenly I saw what it was. Its eyes were unseeing – not blind, but blank. A deranged bear. The perpetually moving body housed a dead mind.

I didn't tell the children about the bear. We continued our walk, they chattered and I answered, and laughed or showed interest, but all the while the bear in a cage at the back of my mind moved constantly.

We went to the zoo as usual the next day and, as we approached the gates, I felt apprehensive, torn between wanting the animal to be there, yet hoping that he was not, in case I should find him still moving, moving, moving, as I had been seeing him since yesterday.

He was still there, and still pacing back and forth.

As I watched I became tense and anxious, more than ever wanting him to stop, just so that I knew he could, yet, for all the fifteen or twenty minutes I stood there, he never hesitated in his one flowing figure-of-eight movement.

As I turned to leave, I saw the old African coming to the pit area. His brows were drawn together, his shoulders a bit bowed – nothing of the old warrior, just an aged servant with something on his mind. I felt I ought to speak.

'You've come again too.'

'Yes, M'em.'

We were both silent, watching the bear.

'It knows nothing of out here.' Indicating anywhere outside the pit. 'This animal is too long in this cell. It wish to go to the ice country and is keep in this city. It is sick in the heart.'

Yes, truly, the bear was sick, heart and head.

On weekends Sara went to stay in Soweto and John and I took the children picnicking along with other company contract families, so I didn't see the Ice Bear again until Monday.

The old man was already there, standing just as I had last seen him, preoccupied, staring blankly down into the pit. I said 'hello' but he didn't look up and soon I too stood silently, willing the bear to drop down, slow down, at least change the rhythm of its three steps and turn, three steps and turn.

I told John about the bear, but when I put it into words it sounded like any story about animals in zoos and circuses. I wanted to explain about the sickness in the heart, and talk about the old man. Later that evening, John was reading the newspaper. 'Listen,' he said, 'your bear's in the paper.' He read out a letter asking why the zoo authorities were keeping the animal in such appalling conditions.

I never understand why people who are quite indifferent to human suffering respond so fiercely to press reports about animals, but they always do. Overnight the Ice Bear became the *cause célèbre* of the moment, so that on Wednesday when I went to the pit there were about thirty people squeezed in front of the cage. The old man and I hadn't a chance, and I felt annoyed, it was our bear. All that I could see was a glimpse of bouncing yellowish fur that puffed up and down as his muscles worked in perpetual motion. The old man was at the far side of the clearing. I couldn't get to him. I thought that he looked once in my direction and I raised my hand, but he looked through me.

In the days that followed, the indignant rumpus in the press grew louder. Reporters and photographers descended upon the zoo demanding that the authorities account for themselves. Which they did. They told how the bear had been rescued from a travelling show which had trundled the creature about Africa in the small cage. Veterinary surgeons and animal psychologists had tried every kind of treatment and given it all sorts of environments, but had found that the least stressful place for the bear was in the pit in the cage in which it had spent most of its life.

But that was not enough. Animal Lovers Protest! Anger at Bear Pit! Zoo Must Act!

And act it did. They shot the bear.

While all this was going on, we still went to the zoo each afternoon, but I kept away from the pit and the sightseers. But as soon as the bear was dead so was the sensation. I knew the cage would be empty yet I had a compulsion to go there.

The pit was empty. There was no reason why he should come, but I had assumed that I would see the old African, and soon I heard the dot of his wooden staff and the shuffle of his ill-fitting shoes. Grey-skinned, droop-shouldered, he stood leaning heavily on his staff. An old man sick at heart.

Ever since that hot February, I have kept locked in my mind the double image of the Ice Bear and the old African. When I am asleep the bear paces obsessively and the old African stares with blank eyes. I used to think that if I wrote about them, brought their images to life, I might finish with them, and I think that I now see the bear only as the great, beautiful tragic animal that it was.

But what about the old African? I had wanted to ask him about himself, about the sickness in his heart, but I never did. He was a boy, a Bantu, a native person, and I was a Baas's lady, IBCC executive wife on contract. I had promised that I would never get . . . involved.

What I might have asked him, and what he might have told me I don't know, for I didn't get involved. I had stood beside him but had said nothing. We both stood there, each inside the cage of our separate skins.

2 THE MANDELA WALL

New York subway graffiti are astounding in their volume, but nowhere is there anything approaching the wall messages of Johannesburg for size and impact. Often a single word: 'Soweto' perhaps, or 'ANC', done with a wide brush in black paint. 'Sharpeville' painted along the entire length of a factory wall; 'Freedom' on a long stretch of suburban pavement.

When I first stepped out on to the balcony of my new

flat, I saw on a thirty-yard stretch of white stucco wall surrounding an old block of flats opposite, 'Nelson Mandela'.

That first summer, I spent a lot of time on the balcony, breaking myself in to the altitude and heat. Below was a garden, landscaped with jacarandas, bougainvillaea and scaled-down kopies and vivid green lawns, entirely dominated by the Mandela Wall across the road. Once, half a dozen men with cans of whitewash came and obliterated the name, and for a few days the wall showed only ninety square yards of brilliant white. Within a week the wall was as readable as ever. Then somebody added a clenched-fist symbol.

During the day, apart from a few aged memsahibs who never ventured out, I was the only white resident. African cleaners padded about all day, quite willing to stop for a mug of tea. I got to know all the gossip, particularly from David, a hump-backed Zulu cleaner, fount of knowledge and carrier of gossip; willing to talk all day if he could get away from the eye of the concierge. But I could not get anything much out of him about the wall.

'When was it done?'

'Some long time now.'

'Who do you think did it?'

A grin. 'Who knows, M'em?'

Indeed, who would know? And if anybody did know they were unlikely to let on to a M'em. But it didn't stop me speculating, wondering about those brave ones who painted the message. Not only was it a subversive act, it must have been difficult to accomplish because the wall ran along the main road from Johannesburg to Pretoria, which was well-lit and overlooked by two blocks of flats.

One day David exchanged a mug of tea and piece of Dundee cake for the rumour that a new block of flats was going to be built opposite and, as usual, David's rumour became fact. Before long all the tenants of the old block had moved out and a demolition crew moved in and, within a few weeks, all that remained standing was the wall. I watched the new building rise with the speed that can be achieved in a wealthy city with a large pool of cheap labour. Within months there stood opposite a twin to the block in which we lived, enclosed by the Mandela Wall.

One January morning, before John or the children were awake, I was watering plants on the balcony. It was not long after dawn and already the air was beginning to feel used and I guessed that by ten o'clock the temperature would be in the high nineties again. Opposite, the daily routine on the building site was starting. The crumpled African night-watchman left his packing-case hut and unchained the corrugated-iron gate which bucked and jerked as it crashed open.

The tinny bell of a wooden chapel was bonging the hour when a lorry came speeding on to the site and braked to a gravel-spraying halt. In the back were some Africans and two black guards, such a gang as one often saw about the city under escort, hard-labouring.

Two uniformed black guards, carrying rhino-tail sjamboks, jumped from the lorry and assembled the prisoners; then, with pushes and shoves, ordered them across the site. They came stumbling, tethered to each other and in single file. A white guard off-loaded some shovels and tools then went to where the tea-boy was brewing up. The prisoners began the demolition of the Mandela Wall.

As usual when something is happening, people stopped to have a look, usually a group of three or four – mostly domestic servants with shopping bags – at any one time. At about eight thirty I noticed an old man. He first caught my attention because he had knotted round him a highly coloured blanket such as many Africans new to the city wear, and carried a knotted bundle. It was obvious, though, that he was quite at home amid skyscrapers, thronging people, traffic, noise and fumes, for newcomers gaze up and all around – as I had done myself not so long ago.

I recognized him from somewhere but could not make the association. I called David to look.

'He's just anybody. Just some old man.'

The old man placed his bundle on the strip of grass between the pavement and the wall and sat beside it. The demolition gang had been working for several hours but the brickwork was so strong and solid that they had not demolished a single letter.

By eleven o'clock the temperature in the shade of my balcony was in the eighties and the air was still. Even the jacaranda tree, which usually responds to every slight movement, was still and quiet, and the air was like thick felt. Roses and cannas looked dark and exhausted, and when the lawn sprinkler was turned on, one could imagine the red earth hissing and crackling. Only proteas and new immigrants in bikinis turned towards the sun.

In that heat the prisoners laboured, and the old man with the bundle sat without shade watching them, moving only occasionally to mop the back of his neck and the lining of his hat. The white guard had gone into the cool, empty flats and the black guards squatted in the shade and sjamboked flies.

At mid-day the building-site tea-boy banged an empty oil-drum. The white guard, wearing only uniform trousers and shirt, emerged from the building and shouted at the gang who threw down their tools and stumbled over to some tin sheds. The man was still sitting beside the wall. Suddenly his name came to me, Kumalo! Mr Kumalo.

Still I could not remember where I had seen him before. Strange that I should know his name, I mean that he was *Mr* Kumalo, for nobody that I mixed with ever used anything but a first name for an African – indeed one couple had said that in all their twenty years in the Republic they had never called their servants anything except 'Jim' or 'Mary'.

I asked all the domestic workers on the first floor if they knew a Mr Kumalo, none of them did. In bed that night I asked John.

'Reverend Kumalo – '*Cry, the Beloved Country*,' he said.

Of course. How odd. Why . . .? Then I remembered where and when I had seen the old man, and why I had associated him with the character in the novel. Both real and fictitious men were Zulu. Rev. Kumalo was 'Inkosi' and I had thought that my man must be a chief, both men had gone downhill. The fictitious Kumalo had wandered about Johannesburg looking for his son and had found him in prison. My old man had spoken of 'sickness of the heart' and of being shut up in a cell.

We had come together briefly, strangely. One afternoon I was in an unfrequented part of the zoo park and had come across a polar bear pacing back and forth, compulsively, in a tiny, grim cage. The old man and I had looked down at the tormented animal. He had asked me about the creature – the 'Ice Bear' he had called it. Until the Mandela Wall, I had not seen him since we had both stood looking at the bear's empty cage after the animal had been destroyed.

That time at the zoo he was obviously going through a bad time and I would have liked to have said something to him, but I had not been very long in the city, did not understand the nuances of apartheid and was afraid to put a foot wrong, so we did not speak except about the Ice Bear.

And now here he was watching those men in the wretched prison gang.

I now knew more about apartheid; the most important thing being that 'Do Not' usually applied mainly to blacks. I became extremely sensitive about asking black Africans anything about themselves, and would have rather been in trouble with the authorities than ask to see a Passbook which on occasion I should have done.

He came every day for two weeks, arriving in the morning and leaving only after the iron gate clanged shut. And every day I made up my mind to go over the road and speak to him and every day I didn't go. Now the only parts of the wall left standing were two brick piers. On the day they were being broken I decided to speak to the old man.

The meeting wasn't easy for either of us. He was courteous, said that he remembered me as the Madam at the Ice Bear's cell. I was awkward and hesitant, knowing that I probably appeared patronizing, and aware that the guards were watching and trying to pretend that they were not.

'You have lost weight,' I said, 'aren't you well?' His head kept up a nodding. Parkinson's Disease or something like that I assumed.

'I am not so young, M'em.'

An awkward silence.

'I live over there . . . I have seen you every day.'

He looked interested.

'I . . . didn't like to come before.'

'There is one there who brings tea. The one . . .' He gestured, humped-backed. He said everything slowly, hesitantly, and I guessed that he had never mastered the difficulties of English and Afrikaans.

'That will be David – he is very kind.'

He kept up the nodding.

'Very kind.'

Another silence.

'Also he allows the use of . . .' He could not find the word so mimed washing his hands, then offered, 'Ablutions?'

We stood again side by side watching torment. He must have made the connection too, but what could he say that would mean anything to a blonde, white-skinned woman, young enough to be his daughter, possibly his grand-daughter, who lived in the air-conditioned glass tower across the road? What could I say to him that wouldn't sound inappropriate or fatuous?

'It is terrible to be in prison – like these men.' And it was fatuous in the utterance.

'It is so. The mind goes sick.'

'Like the bear,' I said.

'The Ice Bear was shot dead.'

'Men jump from prison windows.'

I have never known what to make of the look he gave me then. He started to say something but did not finish the sentence, for one of the black guards strode towards us. He said something to the old man that I did not understand. He looked angry and slapped the rhino-tail sjambok against his bare knees, and appeared to be telling the old man to clear off.

'Leave him alone,' I said. 'He's not bothering anybody.'

'I say to him to stop bothering the Madam.'

'I came to speak to him. He's not bothering me.'

He touched his forehead in salute to me and mumbled an apology; then, turning on his heels military fashion, strode away.

I felt embarrassed for the old man.

'It is the job that he does makes him like that,' I said. 'He's probably all right out of uniform.'

He didn't say anything but just gazed at the last bits of the Mandela Wall being broken down. Still making the association with the Reverend Kumalo of the novel I wondered if this man had been looking for his son. It fitted. David had suggested that the men breaking up the wall by hand, instead of with a bulldozer as the flats had been demolished, were probably political prisoners who were having their noses rubbed in their own handiwork. I guessed that he knew one of the prisoners. Why else had he come day in and day out and sat close to the men doing hard labour?

Our brief exchanges had been about being behind bars, about madness. And now this prison gang. John had recently suggested that staying in this country caused me to suffer from heightened awareness. Nobody comes casually upon characters from novels acting out the plot.

'I have two sons,' I said at last.

He smiled politely, measuring his hand a couple of feet from the ground. 'Small sons?'

I replied with each of my hands at different levels, 'One not so small. Have you some children?'

'Yes, M'em.'

I don't know what pushed me into asking him.

'Is one of them . . .?' I indicated the gang.

'Yes, M'em. I have a son here.' He raised his voice. 'I tell you, M'em, my son is here. I have found him. He ran from his own child. He is . . .' he searched for the English word, 'dog ordure!'

The black guard with the sjambok stepped forward, started in our direction, changed his mind and marched off to the flat that his white superior used as a kind of rest-room.

'I have found my son. What he does is shameful to my

family, my own people.' He was shouting now. 'I pray that the dear Jesus will forgive him, for I cannot. That is the one. Dog ordure!' and he pointed to the black guard with the sjambok.

3 KIZA

'Hey! You, boy!'

Kiza heard her husband's voice.

'Ja, Baas?' The same voice thick with sleep, he answered his own question.

Hidden by the tattered canvas curtain, she heard him stir. Mtolo giggled, excited at the novelty of having Grandfather in the hut, Grandfather who talked loudly in his sleep, and introduced the smell of hand-rolled cigarettes into the hut, a man smell.

She shushed the boy.

'Be quiet. If you cannot do this, then make yourself useful. Go and collect sticks. See that the mealie-pap does not burn. Sweep the yard.'

'Why does he call "Hey! You, boy" and then answer himself?'

' "He"? Who is "He"? Children these days have no respect. When you talk of your grandfather, be respectful.'

'But – he asks questions and answers them himself.'

'You are a chattering monkey. Come and tend the fire.' She tried to put authority into her voice, without success. The boy was the delight of her old age, she kissed the shadow of his footsteps.

Behind the screen, Ngubeni, with stiff movements, pulled on his patched and mended best trousers. To a gecko, bright green against the smoky brown of the hut roof, he said 'Dier – animal', a reflex action from years of translating into the English and Boer languages before speaking.

He tied back the canvas curtain and stood looking about the room which was a cube whose walls were pasted with pages cut from white women's magazines – *haute cuisine* dishes and exotic holiday illustrations being the favourites. A small, enamelled stove, a table and shelves made from soft deal timber, a three-legged stool were pushed back against three walls; on the fourth behind the piece of curtain was the iron-framed bed. On the shelves were displayed those possessions which were prized but seldom used, and several photos in plaster and gilt frames, each gleaming dark face looking very much like the next.

Squatting against the outside wall, Kiza heard him shuffling about, and the small sounds as he touched objects.

'I have come home,' he said, and there in the quiet of the tin hut there were no heads to turn as there had been in the city when he conversed with himself.

'This is my home.' Nodding agreement he went to the washing water and freshened his face and hands.

Not wishing him to know that he had been overheard, Kiza moved away from the wall and approached the hut from a little way off.

'You will have some mealie-pap?' she called.

'A small amount.'

The old woman lowered her eyelids and shook her head. 'Skin and bone. Small amounts! Small amounts!' Tut-tutting she went to a shelf, took down one of the two willow-patterned bowls displayed there, dusted it with her threadbare apron and went into the yard.

The old man followed her and watched as she stirred the porridge pot. The boy, Mtolo, commandeered the spoon and took over, Kiza chiding him in the manner of any grandmother with her favourite grandson.

'Homeland!' said the old man to the open veldt. They looked up from the porridge pot, she indicating to the boy who was ready to comment, that he say nothing.

'Homeland! Why this place? I have never seen this place! I was born in the city.' He addressed the jagged outline of the horizon.

'This wife of mine, she was born in the old township before it was pushed back into the earth. Do you remember the shooting?'

Kiza, not knowing whether he was talking to herself, the mountains or to himself, nodded.

'It is ready for the milk.'

The boy's voice was commanding. Kiza scurried to an earthenware crock covered with a wet cloth and brought out a jam-jar of milk, and they both watched with interest as she poured milk while the boy stirred the mealie-pap. Fussily, she filled the patterned bowl, and Mtolo carried his grandfather's breakfast into the hut and placed it on the sanded deal table.

Kiza and the boy took up places, side by side, on the iron-frame bed that was used as seating during the day, ready to watch the old man eat his homecoming breakfast. He looked into the bowl and sniffed at the steam with pleasure.

'Hmm, proper mealie-pap,' he said.

Kiza looked at Mtolo and nodded, she had told him that that was what Grandfather would say.

The old man was about to start eating when Kiza jumped to her feet and stayed his hand.

'I have lost my brains today.'

The boy giggled. 'You cannot lose something you never had.'

'What are we going to do with you?' she said indulgently.

Ngubeni waited patiently, hot steam rising from the bowl, interest in food returning at the sweet smell.

Kiza took down a tin box. Long ago he had bought it, filled with biscuits, on the morning that they had made their marriage vows at the corrugated-iron chapel in Victoria Township. One of the native stores had marked down the boxes in price to a few cents. The biscuits had been their wedding feast.

On the box lid was a picture of a white king, and she had told her strong, virile husband that she didn't think that the man on the box was much of a king compared with the one beside her. Now, as she removed the lid, she caught his glance for a moment and quickly looked away.

'I forgot the spoon,' she said, and placed one of her best spoons on the table then went back to sit by the boy.

'Grandfather. Are you going to stay with us now?'

The old man pursed his lips and raised his eyebrows suggesting that it was something that he had not much thought about. As though it was a thing about which he had some choice.

'I think I shall stay. I have finished with city life.' He glanced up from his bowl. Kiza concentrated upon the intricate key-pattern on her skirt, tracing the lines with her thumbnail.

'Grandfather. What food did you eat in the city?'

'Mealies. But not good mealie-pap like this.'

Kiza looked at the boy, disappointment showed in his face. Was it so long since Ngubeni had been with children that he had forgotten that small boys do not necessarily want to hear true things? Mtolo wanted the second-hand flavour of city life. He wanted the advertisements he saw in dog-eared magazines at the native store to come to life in the mouth of his grandfather from the city.

'My overseas Madam once gave me a whole Christmas cake to myself. It came from England. In a jet aircraft – from overseas.'

'With white sugar on it?' Mtolo asked, 'and little people, and trees and birds and snow-houses?'

'Yes, like that. Somewhere I believe I still have one of the people.'

Eagerly Mtolo said, 'Can I see it?'

'You may have it to keep.'

The boy looked pleased. 'Thank you, Grandfather. Have you seen snow?'

'One time in winter they made snow statues in the gardens.'

'And was it . . .'

Kiza motioned to the boy to be quiet, and watched the old man who was her husband and whom she scarcely knew. He finished his porridge and then some strong tea, and bread, then sat back and rolled up a cigarette.

Suddenly the boy said, 'Did you find my father?'

Kiza saw that her husband was nonplussed by the question, coming as it did when he was beginning to relax, and coming as it did from the boy. He concentrated on shreds of tobacco.

'Is your father lost then? Did he drop down a crack in the road?'

Kiza shook her head at him. 'He knows that you have been trying to find his father. He is ten years. Old enough.'

Ten years. It was both a long and a short time ago. Ten years since the riots. Ten years since the armoured police vehicle had ploughed into the chanting crowd in the Township killing the boy's mother. Ten years since their son had disappeared into the city. Ten years that she had lived with the boy in this bare land.

The old man nodded to himself.

'I thought the boy was younger.'

'He is old enough.'

Old enough? To know what? To understand what? About truth, honour, loyalty to one's tribe. Her husband's head kept up its nodding.

Kiza wondered if this was the beginning of some affliction of age, the shaking that came to some people.

The old man ran the tip of his tongue along the cigarette paper, rolled it and pinched off the ends, then lighted the tobacco and rested his back against the hut wall.

Again Kiza started tracing the key pattern, and pulling at odd frayed threads . . .

The old awkwardness between them.

They had been married for thirty years, made children, yet there had not been many days in total that they had spent together. There was always this period of readjustment, a strangeness between them, a tension. It was the same for other women who for most of their lives worked in the cities as servants until their joints grew too stiff to kneel to polish and scrub; who lived separate lives from their men; who were heads of their families – until the men returned, and they had to step down.

'How are the bones?'

Kiza looked up at him, puzzled, not understanding how his thoughts had got from talk of the boy's age to 'how are the bones?'.

'The arthritis bones . . . do they hurt you still?'

'It is a drier air in this place . . . they get no worse.' She kneaded her knuckles, wondering if she had in any way shown her resentment at his intrusion into her life with the boy.

Now she waited quietly for him to answer the question

that the boy had asked. He would speak when he was ready.

She had known for several years that their son, the fine handsome son who had been her husband's pride, had not disappeared into the city, had not, distraught with grief, gone to take revenge upon the driver of the police vehicle who had driven into Mtolo's mother as she suckled the baby and watched the protest gathering of schoolchildren. This was what Kiza had told the boy when he had needed something to boast of.

'When they killed my mother in the riots, my father went out to kill the ones who did it. When he has done the revenge he will come and I will live with him,' he could say.

There was no reason to tell him that his father had gone to join his city wife who also suckled his children. No point in saying that he had joined the city police, or to say that she had once seen him. He had been in uniform, armed and carrying a sjambok. He was the native guard of prisoners in leg-chains, men of their own tribe. No reason to say that his father worked in that prison where people jump from high windows because of the things that are done to them.

But men are different. They thought it womanish to hide from truth. Kiza knew that the old man, before finally leaving the city, had gone looking for their son. If she had her way she would have left matters where they were. What good would it do the boy to know? He had little enough to give him pride as it was, being brought up by such a poor shred as herself, in this place that the white baas law had said must be their home.

'The boy is very like him.' His face was turned to the boy, but his words were for her. 'I searched the city for many days.'

He relit the skinny cigarette and leaned back. Kiza saw him well – an old man.

The boy leaned forwards on his elbows. Kiza saw pleasure light her husband's face. His rich voice had not aged and it hit the walls of the hut like drumming.

'I was shown a picture of a man whose features were exactly those of your father – a little older, fatter, but the same. They said that he had gone to another state, which I think is Lesotho. Some said that he had become a famous leader of freedom-fighters. A general! Some people say that he is the one who will return to give freedom.'

The boy's eyes shone. He got up and went to lean close to his grandfather, and Kiza knew that she had lost him to the men. But – she picked up the dishes – Ngubeni had made a concession to this new life that they must now lead together under the one roof, he had softened a little. Told an untruth, kindly, like a woman. Well, that was something.

He followed her into the yard.

'I have brought you this. It is a new headscarf with a picture of the city.'

WOMEN ARE BLOODY MARVELLOUS!

WOMEN ARE BLOODY MARVELLOUS!

JANUARY

January 16th

Carlton Hotel
Johannesburg

Dear Mum and Dad,
Just a picture postcard to say we've landed and are all right. Straight from the great freeze into mid-summer.

Thank goodness we shall not be in this hotel for long. You don't even have to be the idle rich to be idle rich here – if you see what I mean. IBCC with their usual efficiency have provided everything. The children have even got a nanny. Honestly!

The papers are full of new flats for sale so we should soon find something. I will write very soon,

Love, Liz

Dear Grandma and Grandpa,
I did not like flying. I was sick at Rome and sick at Luanda.

This is a picture of our hotel. I like being in a hotel. There is a lady here who plays with us. She is nice. She always wears a hat. She gives Brendan his bath. I bath myself.

Love from Simon

Dear Grandma Burford,
There is a nice lady here who gives us our dinner. I read comics to her. There is a man who cleans our shoes. Dad has got a big new car. Daniel drives it. Daniel has gold buttons. Daniel calls Dad the Master. Daniel calls me Little Master. He calls Brendan Little Little Master. I worked out that I shall be nine when we go back to England, (6+3=9).

Love from Simon

January 17th — Carlton Hotel
Johannesburg

Dear Stell,
No trouble with immigration. Apparently BOSS has a reputation for being extraordinarily inefficient, and unimaginative, so that it wouldn't occur to them that an IBCC company wife could possibly be at all 'political'.

Anyway, it's a super hotel but the sooner we're out the better. In just a few days the kids have taken to being waited upon hand and foot. I can see many a battle on the horizon.

I looked for some mention of your court appearance at Newbury in the *Guardian* but there was nothing – what happened?

Please, please, write and write. I shall hardly bear three years of this isolation from you all.

Sorry to be so brief, but I must write to John's mother. (Do you remember her? The lady who came with me on the Hyde Park demo. She kept calling that policeman 'me duck' and he finished up calling her Jessie.)

Tie a ribbon on the fence for me.

In sisterhood, as they say in *Spare Rib*.

Liz

January 16th

Carlton Hotel
Johannesburg

Jessie,
Thought you'd like this postcard. Those beautiful golden mountains in the distance are pit-tips – it's true – spoil from the gold mines. Jet-lag, hot sun and a home to find, so this is all for now. I shall write up all the local colour for you as soon as there's time.

Love, Liz

January 21st

Cherry Hinton
Aylchester, Hampshire

Dear Liz and John,
The picture postcards were an eye-opener. I hadn't realized it was such a big city.

I know that when you were at university you got mixed up in some sort of protests about South Africa and all that, and I must admit I was worried when you decided to go, especially now you have taken up with all the CND and feminists.

I know you say IBCC don't know that you go on marches and all that, but you ought to be careful. You could ruin John's career. Also, from what I hear you can soon find yourself in trouble out there if you say anything they don't like, and they can keep you locked up without a trial.

I hope you won't get mixed up in anything while you are out there. Remember you have got children now and you have to put them first, no matter what you see that you don't like. After all it's their country and they've got to sort it out.

Take care and don't go out too much in the sun at first. Get some big sun hats for the children – to keep the backs of their necks cool.

Much love, Mum

FEBRUARY

February 7th

2 × 5 Avenue
Clipton, Nottingham

Dear John and Liz,
I'm just blessed fed up with this weather you are best off out of it.

Our David and Jean flew off to Australia on Friday. Now you're all out of the country. Four lads, four daughters-in-law, scattered over the world. And I'm glad. I told our lads, right from when they were little to get shut of this place, it's all The Pit and The Club. I'm glad they've got out. I reckon I shall have to adopt somebody else's grandchildren.

That's how the world seems to be these days. It used to be a lot different when I was young – still, you can't stop progress can you. If it wasn't for my leg and a few other bits and pieces that are wearing out, I think I would be off as well.

I am glad you have got out of that hotel and have got a flat. Children don't like being cooped up.

Your new flat sounds very nice what with three toilets and all that. One day I'll tell you what Alf Dunkin said about people who have three of them – it wouldn't look too good on paper.

I must say the waste from the gold mines makes better-looking pit-tips than this lot round here. Not that they'll be any less mucky for anybody who lives near them, and it's all one to the men who work on the face.

I never thought I'd see the day when one of our lads had a uniformed chauffeur. I know you don't go much on being waited on and that, but I reckon it knocks spots off scrubbing floors.

Send me a bottle of that sunshine. We could do with some here.

Love, Jessie

MARCH

March 7th

101 Chaucer Hall
Illova, Johannesburg

Dear Mum and Dad,
It's been ages since I wrote a proper letter – sorry, but there's been such a lot to getting this place straight, buying furniture, carpets, etc. and, although March is about equal to September back home, the days are still very hot.

The only reason I have time to sit here writing to you this morning is because Brendan is being taken care of by Sara. Who's Sara? Sara is quite a woman: she has infiltrated the Burford household, and I'm at loss to know quite what to do about her. It happened like this.

A few days ago, quite late, she came knocking on the

door looking for a job. She said she must have work with an 'Overseas Madam' because she wanted to learn to be an English cook, and she would work as a maid if I would take her on. I said that I did my own housework, and in any case most of the work was done by the cleaning staff.

She put forward every argument under the sun as to why I should take her on, that she was a devout Christian, had a glowing reference from a Reverend somebody or other, years of experience, etcetera, etcetera, but I kept insisting that I didn't want any help.

Talk about foot in the door! She said she had come all the way from one of the Townships, miles out of town, because she had heard that the concierge of these flats wanted to find somebody for the New Overseas Madam (meaning me) who was in need of servants.

The cheek of it! Me, in need of servants! This concierge has been constantly pestering me about taking on maids, nannies, cooks, and I made it perfectly plain that I had no intention of having servants. She implied that as Chaucer Hall is a very superior type of establishment, people who don't have at least two servants rather lower the tone of the place.

Anyway, as Sara said she had come all the way from Soweto Township, I asked her to come in and have a sit down and a cup of tea.

Well, she came in. She took over making the tea, washing up and putting away. She seemed ever so nice, but I ought to have known about the dangers of 'personal contact' – American service personnel are trained never to see actual women at Greenham, just subversives, which is why they aren't allowed to talk or have 'eye to eye' contact. That's what I should have done with Sara.

After she had gone I noticed she'd left her bag in the kitchen, and I guessed that I hadn't seen the last of her.

Next morning when I opened the door to collect the post, she was waiting outside (in cap and apron if you please). Bubbling over with chatter – she took over the kitchen again. She has been here ever since.

She says she particularly wants to work in this area, so I have agreed that she can stay here as a base while she finds herself a job.

She keeps gathering Brendan up in her arms and hugging him. Brendan seems delighted to have somebody who will play with him all day.

As I write I hear them having a whale of a time playing in the sandbox.

I have a feeling that she could be trying to take us over.

Love, Liz

March 8th

Mother,
Do not send any more letters to this old Township address. I have found an Overseas Madam. If I can make her keep me I can learn English cooking. It will be then that I shall get more money and will not have to be a maid or nanny any more.

She has never had a girl or cook before. She says that Overseas people do not have any servants.

She says I must not eat by myself in the kitchen. She says I must eat with the family. I would not know what to do to sit at table with the Baas. I would be so shy. Therefore I say I do not like to eat except in the evening. This is true as you know. The Madam has said I can stay until I find other work. I think she will not send me away. There is just also only the Baas, Simon who goes to school and one baby who is name Brendan.

I will put some money in this letter. I cannot send much

now. When the new Baas pays me I shall send more. I have to keep a little money to last until the Baas pays me. I am sure he will let me stay. I will then send money for you to buy a dress for Esther.

Tell her to learn everything that the Reverend Ototi teaches her. She cannot become a teacher or doctor without reading and writing and sums.

Your loving daughter, Sara

March 9th

Concierge's Office
Chauccer Hall

Madam,
I am informed by my Head Boy that you have a maid who is sleeping in the non-European servants' quarters.

When your lease was signed I was informed that you did not intend to take up the option on the servant's room allocated to your flat. If my information is correct, will you please sign the agreement.

Doreen Blackmoor, Concierge

March 10th

Flat 101

Dear Mrs Blackmoor,
In reply to the note about the servant accommodation, we do not intend taking up the option on this. The woman you mention is not my maid, she is only on the premises until she finds work. She tells me that she has a friend who works in Flat 89 with whom she is staying temporarily.

Liz Burford

March 10th

Concierge's Office
Chauncer Hall

Dear Madam,
I have spoken to the girl Sara who informs me that she is employed by you as a cook. Will you please confirm in writing whether she is employed by you or not.

You cannot expect another resident to pay rent for a room and your girl staying there.

If she is living on the premises illegally then I must inform the authorities, she is not permitted to stay with any other person employed in this building.

Mrs Doreen Blackmoor, Concierge

March 10th

Dear Mrs Blackmoor,
I had no idea that it was either improper or illegal for a servant to have a friend stay for a few days. To put things on a proper footing, please take this as a formal request to lease the servants' accommodation allocated to this flat, for a period of one month.

Liz Burford

APRIL

April 1st

Newbury Magistrate's Court

Dear Liz,
As you see from the address, it's trouble again. This time I've been charged with 'Obstruction'.

I'm at the camp almost permanently now. It seemed futile assing around as we were. The odd visit. An occasional sing at the gates. Would you ever go the whole thing? I think the Jekyll and Hyde persona was beginning to tell wasn't it? How long could you have kept separate the Liz Burford in the woolly hat and green wellies, and the one in the smart suit and hair-do. Not that I think anybody in IBCC would ever imagine you to be anything other than the model director's wife you were when you boarded the plane. So entirely respectable and establishment.

And what's this about a servant problem? Well at least you won't feel out of things at cocktail parties any more. Your very own servant problem. Wow!

Damn! We are being called into the court now. Fines all round again I expect. My old man is getting a bit edgy these days – doesn't like his name in the paper so I'm pleading in my old name, I quite like it, makes me feel that I own myself again. Must go dear Liz, in sisterhood as they say.

Stell

April 101 Chaucer Hall

Dear Grandma and Grandpa,
We have somebody else living with us now. Her name is Sara. She is a Swazi. Mum says she is not a servant. Marnie De Kloof, who is my friend at school says she is. A lot of people here have servants. She gives Brendan his bath. Sara lets him splash and only laughs at the mess. She is nice. She cleaned my shoes but Dad says she must not. Sara does not give me a bath. I can wash my own hair. Thank you Grandpa for the pocket money.

Love from Simon

P.S. If you would write to Sara she would like it. She does not get letters.

April 15th

Cherry Hinton
Aylchester, Hampshire

Dear Sara,
I hope you don't mind me calling you Sara, I don't know what your other name is. My grandson does seem very pleased that you live with them now. My daughter too writes very highly of you. She has always got on with everybody.

I keep a Birthday Book with everybody I know in it. When is your birthday?

Will you ask Simon to take a photo of you and send it to me?

I have been worrying about my daughter. But now that you are living with them, you will be able to tell her how to go on in that country so that she won't break any rules and get into trouble.

With best wishes,

May Johnston

April 25th

c/o 101 Chaucer Hall

Dear Overseas Grandmother,
I was surprised to have a letter from you. I was very happy to have it. I have never had a letter from England, thank you. I expect it was Simon. He is always writing me letters so that I get some also when the Madam gets the post. Simon is such a sweet child. Brendan too of course. I have learn him to say some Swazi words which make the Baas laugh.

In reply to your question, I have not got a birthday. I

was Christened into the Church May thirtieth. Perhaps this could be my birthday.

My real home, where my mother is, is Orange Free State. This is many hundred miles, it takes two days on trains to get there. Which is how long it take the Madam to get to you.

I shall take great care of the Madam and Brendan and Simon. The children make me very happy.

I shall tell my mother that you have written to me. She cannot write as she did not have school. Her priest writes for her if it is important. I have school until I am twelve years.

The Madam is teaching me to make the Dundee cakes which the Baas like and are not in shops in this place.

Yours faithfully, Sara

MAY

May 3rd

Fifth Avenue
Clipton

Dear Lizzie,
I'm not writing to John and the children, just you.

You sound that bothered about what people will think about Sara working for you. Well, you know what I think – I haven't met a deal of people whose opinion I care tuppence about.

Women have got to look after themselves in this world. It's men who can have ethics and ideals, and what not. I've told you about that time when I black-legged in the General Strike and got my bus turned over. And the time when I brought out all the mill-girls on strike. Well it wasn't because of any ideals – after all I was on a different side of the fence each time. I did what I had to do at the time. I black-legged because I needed the money, and I started the strike because of rotten conditions.

What I'm saying to you is – if Sara needs you and you need her, then to hell with what anybody thinks. It's the blessed men that's the trouble with the world. In my time I've had eight of them to do with one way and another, I reckon I know what I'm talking about.

I've been saying it for years, and I shan't alter, women are bloody marvellous – they should leave us alone to run the world.

Love, Jessie

May c/o 101 Chaucer Hall

Mother,

The Overseas Baas has given me money to buy clothes and furniture, so I send an extra ten rand, and Esther can have a new dress and socks also. These socks are for church only.

I have a room without sharing with another girl. Some of these girls want also a room for their own and make trouble. The Concierge Madam is cross with me because of it, and This One she tries to catch me out and is inspecting my room always. She is looking always for signs that I have boys in my room. She will not get me dismissed this way for never will I have any of them.

The Baas says we shall soon go to Durban for a holiday. It is not usual to go in May, but the Baas does not like hot weather.

Many Overseas Baases come to the flat but they do not wish to eat English food. My Baas likes only English food. The Madam is letting me do some cooking. I do not like to have another woman in my kitchen, but the Madam is always there. It is very strange, for it is now like I am a proper cook and the Madam is the kitchen-maid.

I tell her she should go to work in an office like all the other Madams. If she went to work I could have the kitchen to myself. She says I can stay here only if we share the work, even though she so much does not like housework.

I have said to her that you would not catch me doing House Boy's work, so then why does she wish to do maid's work? That is different, the Madam says.

She comes into my kitchen all the time and tells of England. It is interesting, but I like my own kitchen. I do not understand her ways. She talks a lot of politics and that sort of things. I do not understand why she bother with this. She has all things – except her own people, who she misses very much.

Tell Esther that she must not miss even one day without learning some reading or writing. I want very much for her to have a good job when she is a woman. I will never let her be a servant. Tell her this. I shall send postcards from Durban.

Your loving daughter, Sara

The Blue Marlin Hotel
Amanzimtoti, Durban

May

Dear Jessie,
It is out of season but the weather's like a balmy English spring. We swim and sunbathe, and write very short letters.

When people realize that you are a newcomer, they always ask what you think about their country. I usually say 'It's absolutely beautiful', but that isn't what they mean. What they really want is approval of their lifestyle.

Why do those who have the cake not want anybody else to have any, not even the crumbs? I should like to ask why they can't see that they don't have to go on clutching their loot to their bosoms like dying misers, it's a country even richer than ours – and that's saying something, isn't it.

But I promised my Mum I wouldn't get involved whilst I'm out here.

Poor old John, it's worse for him, mixing with big business all the time. He's just not IBCC material. It won't last for ever, that's one thing.

This country – ah but it's beautiful though. If things were different I could happily live here for the rest of my life.

May

The Blue Marlin Hotel
Amanzimtoti

Dear Auntie Stell,
Kom gou! Kom kyk! Daar is die berg. We all have to learn this language at school. It means come quick and see the mountain. We came through mountains on our way to Amanzimtoti which is the name of the seaside.

Love from Simon

May

The Blue Marlin Hotel
Amanzimtoti, Durban

Dear Grandma Burford,
I can now read things in two languages. I can read what it says on this beach. It says 'Geen Hound – Geen Swartz' which means that dogs and black people are not allowed. I do not know why they are not allowed except the dogs who make messes everywhere.

Love from Simon

The Blue Marlin Hotel
Amanzimtoti, Durban

Dear Grandma and Grandpa,
Sara liked getting your letter. If she comes with us she is allowed to sit on the beach for white people. Did you know that Sara is black?

If my friend Miki came here he would have to go on the black beach. I am not allowed on the black beach. It is not the sand is black, it means black people's beach.

Miki is not black. Sara says in this country he counts as black. Mum says it is because they have different laws here. How can yellow be black, it is silly.

There is no shark net on that beach. We have only seen one person on that beach. Sara says the sharks have eaten everybody else. Sara said it was a joke. It is best not to have dogs on the beach. I think everybody ought to have a shark net.

Some things are not very nice. We saw hundreds of dolphins this morning. They are very nice.

Love, Simon

The Blue Marlin Hotel
Amanzimtoti, Durban

Dear Stell,
It's not easy applying one's mind to answering letters where the flying fishes play (truly I can see some now), but I will try. Just a few thoughts as they come drifting over this splendid white beach and crashing surf.

I worry about my kids. Especially Simon, he's a bright kid and questions everything. Why did we come here? he asks. I don't have an answer he would find acceptable. We're here for the money of course. Future career, job security, children's futures – it still amounts to the same thing. Money! 'We're here because that's how Daddy earns his money.' I should say to him, 'These things are wrong, I'm taking you home', but I won't will I – because of the fear of going back to being poor, because of the mortgage . . . because of the money! A share of the spoils.

Recently he has become quite obsessive about skin colour (which isn't surprising when even park benches are labelled 'black' or 'white'). One of his friends at school back home was a little Japanese kid, and he keeps asking questions about him. Where would Miki sleep? Could Miki go in that door, would he be 'allowed', etcetera, etcetera, and I could cry.

Sometimes I think that I can't stand much more of it. I already drink far more than is good for me. You remember Mildred Layton ginning her way through *The Raj Quartet*? Blotting it out. I'm not that bad but I understand those women a little better now.

As Simon says – some things are not very nice. But then some things are so beautiful that you want to weep. The Draakensburgs, with the sun setting. The Valley of a Thousand Hills, with mists rising. Dolphins leaping in clear blue seas. The more I see of this country, the more I love it, hate it, and feel guilty about being here at all.

Weep! Cry! Guilt! Hate! Such emotion in an IBCC executive-type wife.

And . . . I am shocked at my own prejudice against Afrikaners. I always find my hackles rising when I hear the accent and language. God's Chosen People! They really believe that they are doing God's will. Odd God!

They use their own language, even when they know you cannot understand. Then what happens? You retaliate, using your own. There! You see? Animosity and trouble.

Too much time to think here.

Much love – in sisterhood as they say,

Liz

The Blue Marlin Hotel
Amanzimtoti, Durban

Dear Jessie,
The flowers, the flowers, how you'd love to see them. Banana trees whose black blooms are like 'bird of paradise' flowers in widows weeds, proteas like Muppet Show flowers, and sugar-bushes, proteas, canna lilies.

Sara knows almost no names of trees or flowers, yet she knows things like make of cars. Ah, but she is my salvation. We talk, talk, talk all day. Do you know what – she can speak four languages yet the pinnacle of her ambition is to be an English-trained cook?

I hardly see any white people from morning to night. I have been partially admitted into the sisterhood of black women who live in the flats. We stand at the ends of the corridors exchanging small scandals and gossip. It takes me back to my childhood on the council estate. They accept me because of the one thing we have in common – we are lonely and exiled from our families.

But there can never be any getting away from the fact that I am a white, a madam. No getting away from my skin, my privilege.

Why the hell did I inherit my Grandpa's tendency to be political? It must be great to lie on your back and only see the sky and feel the sun.

Love, Liz

From Durban

Mother,
I think it is true that the illness you have is the kidneys. I send you this sea water. Sea water contains many things that are good for kidneys. Let Esther drink some also. It is good for making pure blood.

I will like it better when we get home to the city. For here I must sleep with all the other girls who work in the hotel.

The food is not good. There are no baths. I use the Madam's bath.

Tell Esther I insist that she tries harder with her reading. If she does not she will grow up to be a servant only. To be a doctor or teacher she must have education. She must understand the need.

Your loving daughter, Sara

Reverend Ototi,
Do not read this part of the letter to my mother. Please write about how sick she is. I am worried that I am so far from her. Please also make Esther do her lessons. Tell her what it is like to have to be a servant. Tell her there is no dignity. Tell her it is not a good life. Thank you and God's blessings.

Sara Mashele

JUNE

Concierge's Office
Chauncer Hall

Dear Madam,
Now that you have returned from your holiday may I ask you to deal with the matter of your girl's room. It is now several weeks since you took over the non-European servant's room temporarily, will you kindly inform me as to whether you wish to lease it on a permanent basis.

Doreen Blackmoor, Concierge

Flat 101

Mrs Blackmoor,
In reply to your note, please let me have the necessary agreement.

Liz Burford

Concierge's Office
Chaucer Hall

Dear Madam,
You are probably aware that it is not usual for one girl to occupy a room to herself. The non-European servants' quarters only provide enough rooms for two girls or two boys per room. If your girl shares it will cost only half what you are paying for her just now. She can share with the girl in Flat 108.

Doreen Blackmoor, Concierge

Flat 101

Dear Mrs Blackmoor,
I wish Sara Mashele to have sole occupancy of the room. These rooms are so small that there is scarcely room for one person, let alone two. Sara has her furniture and other belongings leaving no space for anybody else.

Liz Burford

Concierge's Office
Chaucer Hall

Dear Madam,
Non-sharing cannot be guaranteed to servants. When all the flats are occupied they will have to share. Two servants to a room is what is provided.

Doreen Blackmoor, Concierge

Concierge's Office
Chaucer Hall

Dear Madam,
I have been informed by some of the Residents of this block that their non-European servants are being unsettled because of the difference in the wages you pay your girl, and the large amount of free time she gets, and having a room to herself.

I have told them that you are new to this country and do not know the problems that come from over-paying servants, and think that you are doing right by paying high wages. If you give them too much money they do not know how to handle it.

Some American Residents who moved in just before you started off like this but have now brought their girl's wages into line with the rest.

If you would like me to call upon you I would be pleased to let you know what is the best way to deal with Bantus and coloureds.

Doreen Blackmoor, Concierge

Concierge's Office
Chaucer Hall

Dear Madam,
Please inform your non-European servant that she must use the back stairs unless she is accompanied by a Resident or in charge of children. The front stairs and the lifts are strictly for the use of Residents.

Doreen Blackmoor, Concierge

Flat 101

Mrs Blackmoor
I understand that you have complained to Sara Mashele regarding push-chair wheel marks in the corridors. As both push-chair and baby are mine, she can hardly be held responsible.

In future, please address all such complaints to myself.

Liz Burford

JULY

IBCC (SA) Pty
Victoria Park Road
Johannesburg
TO
Jubert Properties
Victoria Park Road
Johannesburg

Dear Sirs,
Please take this as confirmation of our telephone agreement to lease a two-person room in the servants' quarters in Chaucer Hall for the use of any domestic servant of our Mr J. Burford.

Yours faithfully, C.J.Exton – Personnel Manager

SEPTEMBER

Orange Gate
Greenham

Dear Liz,
I'm back for a week or two. Some new faces, many familiar ones.

It's not like you to let people like that dreadful woman get you down. I wish we could just sit down quietly and talk. I need it too.

They keep coming in and breaking the camps, and sometimes breaking us, but not our spirit.

If we can't stop the old men in the White House and the Kremlin, what matters skin colour, we shall all be the

same – dappled Nuke.
Come back to us soon. We miss you.

Stell

P.S. Gerry and I are breaking up. It's not much of a marriage now I'm so much involved here. Poor old Gerry, he deserves better, but there's no going back is there, once you've committed yourself.

NOVEMBER

c/o 101 Chaucer Hall

Mother,
The Baas said that I should go home to stay with you for Christmas. I said to him that I wish to cook Christmas food in the flat. If I am to be a trained cook I must learn this.
Tell Esther I shall listen to her reading when I come home. This will be at the end of November.

Your loving daughter, Sara

Cherry Hinton
Aylchester, Hampshire

Dear Liz and John,
It must seem funny having summer in November. Fancy having Christmas dinner in the sun. It would seem funny to me I must say.
In those newspapers you sent, there did seem to be a lot about shooting in them. It said there was a man shot outside Chaucer Hall. Dad said it probably wasn't the

same place, as you live in the better parts where that kind of thing would not happen.

Do the police out there carry guns? Are there any black policemen? I can't help worrying about you. If all those things are happening it must be like Starsky and Hutch or something.

Things seem very cheap. I hope it doesn't tempt you to smoke and drink too much.

Much love, Mum

Oh, Mum. Yes, what Starsky and Hutches. I have seen them (yes here in this 'best part'), seen a struggle between a detective with a gun and an African with a jagged bottle. Heard shots fired in the next block of flats. Yes, there are black policemen – strutting like their white counterparts, striking out with sjamboks at prisoners in chains. Yes things are cheap. Brandy is cheap, cigarettes are cheap, labour and meat are cheap, and of course the sun is absolutely free. The Good Life!

101 Chaucer Hall
Illova

Dear Mum,
You do seem to have picked out the worst bits. You get violence in any city. A lot of the trouble is because workers come to the city without Passbooks. The police are always rounding them up and sending them away. They soon come back, because they have to work somewhere.

This is a big city – not darkest Africa. There are shops like Marks and Sparks and Woolies here. Mum, please don't worry so . . .

DECEMBER

NOTICE TO ALL RESIDENTS

SIR OR MADAM,
WOULD YOU KINDLY INFORM YOUR NON-EUROPEAN SERVANTS THAT AS FROM TODAY (DECEMBER FIFTH) NO VISITORS WILL BE ALLOWED IN THE BUILDING. ANYONE FOUND IN THE NON-EUROPEAN QUARTERS WITHOUT A PERMIT, WILL BE ARRESTED FOR TRESPASSING. POLICE ARE ASKING FOR ALL CITIZENS TO COOPERATE IN THE FIGHT AGAINST TERRORISTS. PLEASE SEE THAT YOUR SERVANTS DO NOT BRING UNAUTHORIZED PERSONS ON TO THE PREMISES.

Doreen Blackmoor, Concierge

Concierge's Office
Chaucer Hall

Dear Madam,
In reply to your enquiry. To clarify the rules, friends and relatives of non-Europeans are not permitted to visit these premises on any pretext whatsoever. The new rule means that only Residents' servants and my own staff are allowed on the premises. This must be done to protect ourselves and our children from terrorists and natives who belong to illegal organizations.

I now carry a firearm, and my staff have been instructed to inform me of any person who is on the premises illegally.

Doreen Blackmoor

c/o 101 Chaucer Hall

Mother,
I have got back here. I told you that it was not necessary for you to worry. I did get Esther safely into my room without the Concierge Madam seeing her. Mabel Nguma was waiting for me as she had said and helped me to hide Esther. Esther is now sleeping.

At once when I arrived I told the Madam the truth that I have a child. It was a great surprise to her. She cried some when I tell her that I bring Esther to live with me because of your sickness. She has said that I must write at once to let you know that all is well so that you will not worry.

I know that you will miss Esther as she has been your baby more than mine. Also Esther does not know me as her mother. She will soon get used to this.

The Baas is in England for a few days. The Madam is making very many telephone calls about Esther, also she says we must hide Esther until she gets the right papers. She says we must trust only Mabel. The Madam has always like Mabel.

I am sorry that you did not tell me a long time before this that you were so very much ill. I will come home to visit very soon. I must first get papers for Esther to live in the city. The Madam says she will surely get papers because she is my child and that there is now no one is at home who can look after her. I think the madam will fix things for us. Baases from the City Council come often to have dinner with my Baas and Madam. They will know what to do.

Please mother, do not worry any more. You must get well.

Your loving daughter, Sara

101 Chaucer Hall
Illova

TO The Department of Native Affairs
Dear Sirs,
Can you please tell me how to proceed to obtain a permit for a non-European servant to bring her child to live in the city?

Yours faithfully, E. Burford (Mrs)

Department of Native Affairs
Carlsburg Place, Johannesburg

Dear Madam,
Reference to your letter of December seventh, I have to advise you that no such permits are available.

Yours faithfully, Kobie Van Rensburg
p.p. C. Cotzee

Dear Sirs,
Can you please give me some advice on how to proceed regarding the child of a non-European . . .

Dear Madam,
The issue of any permit, pass, etc. is entirely dependent upon age, and other considerations.

At the age of fourteen, if a Working Permit is being sought then you should write to . . .

Dear Sir,
Can you advise me . . .

Dear Sir,
Can you please give me some advice . . .

Dear Sir,
Can you please advise me . . .

Dear Madam,
We are unable to advise you . . .

Dear Madam,
We would refer you to the attached leaflet DBA44 paragraph 145N wherein it is stated that 'no dependent child or children of non-European workers . . .'

Dear Madam,
In reply to your enquiry. There is no provision made . . .

Department of British Affairs
Temporary Residents' Department

Dear Madam,
Your letter to the British Ambassador has been passed to me.

I am instructed to inform you that we are unable to offer any assistance.

This is a matter for the non-European Administration, and we would suggest that the non-European worker in question makes enquiries.

Yours faithfully, Brian C. Keough,
Administrative Assistant

Parkwood

My Dear Mrs Burford
Your letter to the Bishop's Palace has been passed to me as the matter is not something which the Bishop can properly deal with.

I regret that I can offer little real help, and whilst I appreciate your concern, there seems to be nothing we can do but offer the suggestion that you write to various appropriate bodies.

With regret that I am unable to help.

Yours sincerely, Jacob Mansbridge

101, Chaucer Hall

HAPPY CHRISTMAS

Dear Stell,
Hard to believe, but it is Christmas afternoon. It is ninety in the shade, and we are harbouring an illegal immigrant. You would think it was an escaped convict or a terrorist, the great carry-on there's been.

Actually I believe I could cope with that situation better than this one. This immigrant – this illegal immigrant – illegal child, is a bony little ten-year-old in a frilly skirt and pink hair-ribbons . . .

JANUARY

c/o 101 Chaucer Hall

Dear Overseas Grandmother,
Thank you for the New Year present you have sent to Esther.

It has been very worrying for us. I would never bring this trouble to the Madam. The Baas knows many city official people, I thought it would be easy to fix. Esther is my child and there is no one else who she can live with.

The Madam has written to everybody and made many

phone calls. They say Esther must go away, which means that I also must leave. Then how would we live, I left Kimberley because I could not get work there to keep Esther and help my mother.

Right from when they are born children are hard to care for and to make them grow up well. It is always hard for the mothers.

Esther's father is a teacher and I want for her to have some good future like his. I do not know where this man is now. I do not want to know him. He was my teacher and I am pregnant when I am still at school.

My mother is dying. Never has she had one day without the worry of children. When she was just young she was a nanny. Then her own children. I have six brothers and sisters. It is always like this for the old people, when sons and daughters go to the cities to find work the old people must care for the grandchildren.

The Madam and I many times have talked about all the things in the world to put right. If the world could be made better just now . . . it would be too late for my mother.

Yours sincerely, Sara Mashele

Cherry Hinton
Aylchester, Hampshire

Dear Liz,
The letter from Sara broke my heart. What worries me is that you will do something silly and start getting yourself into trouble. It's no good you putting Simon and Brendan at risk no matter how terrible you think it is for Sara's little girl.

I wish John had never been sent out there. I just hope that he is being level-headed about it all. I just hope he

gets his job done and gets back home as soon as he can.
I will write more when Auntie Nance has gone back.

Love, Mum

FEBRUARY

2 × 5 Avenue
Clipton, Nottingham

Dear Liz,
Your last letter was a bit of a jumble. You said that Sara had gone to join the women in the cathedral, but you didn't say that they were starving themselves as a protest. It wasn't until I saw the piece in the *Observer* that I understood. I remember what my own Mam told me about force-feeding the Suffragettes. I hope they don't do that to them.

Give Sara my love and tell her that I think she's bloody marvellous.

Jessie

From outside St. Joseph's Cathedral

Dear Stell,
I have to tell you as much as possible about what is happening here. It is important that you know so that you can tell others. I believe that there has been almost total indifference back home, to what is happening.

I don't know whether Sara knew about the protest before she brought Esther here, and it doesn't matter. What matters now is that she is involved.

The women could easily die, and you must tell as many people as you can. I get the English papers and there has been almost total silence (or indifference) to this protest.

This hunger strike is as serious and important as anything prisoners in the Maze have done. Here are mothers starving themselves to death. Quietly with their children around them, whilst the press gives pages to an MP who ought to have got himself vasectomized, and princes . . . who likewise.

At last John has seen the kind of society IBCC and companies like it are supporting. No, that's not true, he's always known but because of this . . . obsession . . . he has about security for me and the kids, he could rationalize what he does. And so could I. Now he wants out.

It's a long time since we have been so close. He has taken leave that is due to him and is at home looking after the children. I am just sitting around outside the cathedral and it is cold. I hardly know why I keep coming. I can do nothing. I only know that I need to be here, to be near these women who are taking on the almighty State.

There are now sixty inside. It is nineteen days since they had any food, and they are determined to continue until the Government agrees to give them the right to live and to bring up their children in the areas where they work.

The children are fed and play about apparently quite happily, but the women are becoming very weak. As I have learned over these last months living closely to Sara – most women who work as servants live almost entirely on starch, sweet tea and junk food, which makes them overweight and lacking in stamina. I wonder how many fences would be pulled down at Greenham if we didn't get our protein and vitamins.

Calm determination is a journalistic cliché; but I tell you, Stell – that's what you see in this cathedral.

In sisterhood dear Stell,

Liz

Greenham

Dear Liz,
'Women, like flames have a destroying power, Ne'er to be quenched till they themselves devour.' It's Congreve – had you heard it before? Not that it's any comfort, but it does seem to be our way doesn't it? Sara's women and the Grannies here who sleep rough in the camps in bitter weather are devouring themselves. Now They are coming in to destroy our camps – legally. We rebuild and they come again. I look at the Grannies at the fence and . . . yes, yes, John's mother is right – women are bloody marvellous.

In solidarity and sisterhood.

Stell

St Josephs Cathedral

Dear Madam,
I am sorry that our time together finishes with so much trouble.

For me the time at the flat was good. You and I, Madam, learned so many things about each other.

All the weeks that I have been here, I have had so much time to talk and listen to the others.

You know that I have always been proud that I am a Swazi. Swazis think we are the most intelligent of all people. And you know also what I have said about the Zulu – loud in the mouth and show-off. And the Baca – the great fools who know how to do nothing but to sing when they collect garbage and to run with their dustbins.

All my life I have live close with girls of many tribes but never like now. Here we are not tribes, we are parents only . . . mothers.

If we die, it will perhaps be that people will look at our bodies and see that servants of all the tribes need to have their children to live near them.

I think that is why this fasting protest is important. If the Government sees that we are people . . . not natives . . . not nigras . . . not Mary or Jim or Hey-boy! or Hey-girl! but sees us as people like all others, then they cannot forbid us our children.

The Bible says that we must not kill our own bodies. But Madam, at last I see that the Bible is full of men's words. Women have no hand in writing it. Always it is the men telling us what God has said. Even that God is man. So perhaps he is, for a woman would perhaps make a more kind world. Madam, I am not now shocked, as I used to be, that you do not believe in any God.

Also I do not now believe that it is sin to kill our own bodies. For us there is no other way.

Yours sincerely, Sara

Dear Sara, I have had a visit from Mabel Nguma. It was a strange meeting. Chattering Mabel who boiled the sweet tea for us in her madam's kitchen, when we gossiped at the corridor ends, called upon me as Mabel the political, intellectual. She said I ought to stay away from the cathedral, that people like me did not help. It must be 'the fight of the mothers' she said. I said to her, I am a mother, but she shook her head. She said that blacks must fight on their own; that when the real fighting starts there would be no time to stop and wonder if the white in the line of fire is a friend. Bullets come out of machine-guns too quick to choose, she said. Perhaps she is right. So, Sara, it is better that I don't come to the cathedral any more. It is better too, that I don't write any of this down. For the first time in my life I feel afraid to write or speak my mind.

MARCH

101, Chaucer Hall

Dear Sara,
I have to tell you that we are going home to England almost at once. My husband is going to teach at a college in England.

Mabel tells me that the Government is sending a Minister to look into the 'illegal children'. At least that shows that they are admitting that you have a valid case and will now have to do something.

You do not need me to tell you how unhappy I feel that I shall not be there to meet you when you leave the cathedral.

In sisterhood and with affection,

Liz Burford

St Josephs

Dear Madam,
I will try to let you know what happens, but already I am so weak. I write often to keep my mind thinking.

Do you remember when we all went to Amanzimtoti and I said why does the Baas not buy a hotel for us to run. We could all live in it and I could cook English food for tourists. The Madam could be in charge and the Baas could build the engineering things if he wanted to. The children could go to the beach every day. Do you remember how the Baas laughed?

It was before you knew about Esther. I thought that she too could live in the hotel and go to school, and then get to be a doctor or a teacher or anything . . . but not a servant.

It is twenty-four days that we have not eaten. Sometimes I am not sure whether the singing is in the cathedral or inside my head.

I shall be sad not to have my Overseas Madam and Baas, and I shall miss Simon and Brendan so much. But Madam for girls like me, always it is like this. Good jobs do not last very long, but bad jobs also do not. We get used to moving on always.

My fingers do not work very well, and I cannot hold a pen, only in my head can I write to you . . .

MAY

Dear Madam,
I have received the letter and money you left with Mabel.

My mother died before we came from St Joseph's. I have not seen her grave.

I cannot give you an address for me, because this place where the women have been sent is not anywhere, and they keep moving us.

In the fourth week of the fast someone came to tell us that the cases of the illegal children would be heard. At first we said that it was not true, that it was a plot to get us out, because if we died it would be bad for the Government. They said that it was true. They said we must trust. A man high in Government was told to listen to us.

It truly was a plot.

We came out of the cathedral. We were brought here in lorries. We make shelters of boxes and sacks but the bulldozers keep coming and coming and we keep building again. We must. We have nowhere to go.

We stay here in this place made of cardboard and sacks. It is now many months since we were brought here. Nothing has been done about our children.

Now that we are not in a cathedral starving to our death, the newspapers and photographers do not come. People who starve in shanty-towns are not news. We should never have come from the cathedral, but let them carry out our bodies for all to see. But we believed them when they said that we had won, that we should be heard.

Mabel got Esther a place in Bethesda Hostel for homeless children. It is near the old city. Mabel says that Esther is now speaking some English and is learning reading and writing. If I get back my Passbook I shall try to get work again in the city so that I may see Esther sometimes.

I am afraid to go to the city until they give me my papers back. Madam, is it not strange how these things turn about. Now that Esther is allowed to stay in the city, it is I who am illegal.

Your friend, Sara

JULY

Bethesda Hostel
Johannesburg

Dear Mother,
You see, I can write. I am learning to cook. Soon I shall

get a job and I can send money for you. I pray for you every morning.

Esther Mashele

FOUND DRUNK IN PARADISE STREET

FOUND DRUNK IN PARADISE STREET

It is Friday. This is the List.

Court Number One
Sitting at the Law Courts, George Street, on the . . . twentieth . . . day of . . . Nov . . . 19 . . .

Informant or Complainant	*Defendant Age or Date of Birth*	*Nature of Offence or Matter of Complaint*
Police	Mary MALLORY	Found drunk in Paradise St.

Mary MALLORY. And eighty-five others.

The Police, the DHSS and the Council. The usual *Informants* and *Complainants*. Familiar names are here. 'Hello, he's been at it again.' The Gross Indecency, the Attempting to Pervert the Course of Justice, the Distraint Warrants, the Driving with Excess Alcohol . . . the Found Drunk.

Mary Mallory you are here again . . . my *bête noire*, my scourge, running sore of my conscience. Always here, brought up from the cells week after week. She appears in many guises, under different names, young and old, cocky and humble. Sometimes she has been shop-lifting . . . stole a pair of velvet curtains from British Home Stores – stole two Porsche Turbo cars together valued at £5.90. Sometimes she has had a go at her neighbour . . . Must show cause why she should not be Bound Over to be of Good Behaviour to Keep the Peace. She keeps me in thrall because she is a woman and I am a woman, and there but for the grace of God and all that kind of thing. And I am kidding myself if I think she cares a damn. I'm THEM and she's US and it's no good me kidding myself that I'm US when she's in the dock and I'm in charge of Court Number One.

Eighty-six offences this twentieth of November.

The Police are Informing against William SMITH, Stephen HOLLOWAY, Susan COLLINS, Jacqueline WILLSON, and the DHSS Complain of Leslie HARRIS, Henry STUART, Barbara CHARLESWORTH and sixteen others who made false statements to obtain supplementary benefit – and pages of A Like Offence. Roy SMITH has exposed his person. William WILLIAMS rode a pedal cycle on a road otherwise than in the specified direction, and the police are Informing the Courts.

Fifty or so citizens who cut up rough . . . well, fifty who were found out, anyhow.

I've never been found out. And that's a lie. But it was a local traffic policeman who stopped me. Don't I know you? He's severe at first, thinking he's booked me before. Yes, I say, Traffic Court. I smile. Recognition shows on his face. To say yes I am a local JP would put him on the spot – like offering a bribe. I smile. Of course, he says. Funny how people look different when you see them in different surroundings. He smiles. I smile. I don't remember seeing him anywhere except in the witness box. He puts his notebook away. He smiles. There might come a day when he's got evidence that is a bit thin and I'm in charge of his case. He plays safe. Uses his discretion. Wags his finger playfully. Well Ma'am, you don't want to have to fine yourself for speeding. We smile. He touches his cap. He does not inform anybody of the Nature of My Offence.

Second busiest court in the country. That's what somebody has just said. A kind of pride, as though we expect one day to win the cup. It gives us importance. Ours is the second in the league of lawless cities. A look at the list is like watching bees in a glass-sided hive. You can see into the little cells of power. The Council is clamping down on Rates Defaulters. The Vice Squad has had a complaint about the lavatories in the Rose Gardens. Somebody in the DHSS decided to have a go at Cohabiting Women.

Barbara Charlesworth. I shall remember you to the day I die. She shouts at us. She is a magnificent twenty stone with two plastic carriers full of shopping. You can all sod off, she shouts. He brought some groceries and some toys for the kids, I never said he didn't. But I never slept with him. They're his kids an't they? There an't nothing wrong with buying your own kids toys is there? And the groceries he bought was for him – if you thinks I can afford to give him his dinner out of supplementary, you must be daft. The Solicitor, mouthpiece for the DHSS, the Complainant, is giving her enough rope. Christ! She even bangs the table. I bang my table in reply. No need to shout Mrs Charlesworth. Miss! she shouts, not Missis – MISS Charlesworth. Yes, he did stop in the house. He slept on the bloody sofa. It was raining and he only had his jacket, what did you expect me to do, tell him to clear off? The DHSS man looks at us expecting to elicit sympathy. He sat outside Miss Charlesworth's house all night, waiting for the father of her children to get on his bike and ride off to work at the docks – they followed him and sent a woman in to tackle her about the illegal cohabiting . . . Pity he's a dockie and not a Lesbian lover paying for the odd bag of groceries and toys out of her good job in the Rates Office. I don't have sex with nobody no more. Christ! I got eight bloody kids already. He slept on the sofa. The DHSS solicitor compliments the good neighbour who informed on Miss Charlesworth in an anonymous letter, asks us what we would do without these concerned citizens . . . and Miss Charlesworth? What would he do without the Legal Aid scheme? On his bike? Down the docks? I'm no good at this job. If I were any good, I wouldn't think like that. The DHSS man is on Special Assignment. Like Store Detectives and other *Informants or Complainants* he believes promotion depends on the number of convictions that are down to him on his file in the Personnel Office.

There was a time, not that long ago either, when a spare communal hat was kept in a dusty cupboard for women magistrates who turned up without one. To do with dignity and respect, the sight of a woman's uncovered hair bringing discredit upon a court, a place of Brylcreem and bald heads. It took a strong lady who spent good money on hair colour to tell them what they could do with their hats. Nobody told me it was a condition of being a Magistrate she said. And nobody had. And it wasn't anyway. So out went hats. It was a legal nicety in the Magistrates' Room. Nobody said she had to wear a hat. You didn't need to refer to a Stone's Justices' Manual to see that she had a good case against hats. That was before my time. It is one of the legends. Something to talk about when solicitors are keeping you waiting, as they juggle the system to get as many fees out of one morning as possible. Legal Aid is a gold-mine for them we say, but what can you do? If you make a fuss . . .

Eighty-six Offences. Number One Court. On a rota basis of senior magistrates, I get the chair, the throne. Who's been sitting in my chair? Five foot one, Goldilocks in Daddy Bear's chair. There have been women JPs for a long time now, but courts are like kitchens, entirely masculine in dimension and concept. In my kitchen I have a little stool to reach the low shelves, and tall men in the family to reach the others. There is a spare foam cushion under the throne for those of us who don't measure up: our shoes fall off, our feet dangle in mid-air, frozen, but from the waist up the dignity of the court is served.

Mary MALLORY Found Drunk in Paradise Street. I avoid her eyes that watch below, in the Bridewell. I'm no good at this job, Mary Mallory. Who do we think we are? Who do I think I am, legs dangling in Daddy Bear's chair, gold crests, fine wood panelling? Fine, dirty, wood panelling. Sunshine opens the raincoat of the court and flashes us the human grime of years. Patches of solicitors' grease, sweat left by speeders, addicts, murderers, rapists, and the thousands who didn't know what came over them Sir/Madam/Your Honour. They hold on to bits of fine wood panelling and mouldings, trying to tell us their side of the story.

In answers. Not the way they would tell it in a pub or over the garden fence. Except just occasionally a Barbara Charlesworth says sod off! and we see for a moment, before the solicitors and Court Clerks jump in and hedge us around with jargon, we see for a moment that here is just another room full of people saying things to one another. Mary Mallory is waiting below not knowing that she might be my last straw. Going soft? Menopause? PMT? Male colleagues understand. Roll their eyes and raise their brows behind my back, they make allowances for women JPs. Once one of them patted my hand, called me A Friday Dove – I could have hit him . . . I should have hit him.

'All stand.'

All obey. Eleven o'clock. In the golden days – before Post Office Clerks, Co-op Managers, Union Convenors and women without hats – there used to be a coffee break. There have been time and motion studies of this court in the Premier League. Coffee is taken during work allocation before opening time. This 'All Stand' is for us to retire to consider the evidence.

'Did you see this?' I say, to exorcize my dread of Mary Mallory. 'Drunk in Paradise Street.'

'I used to live there,' says Uncle Fred, Grand Old Man, due to retire.

'Thought they pulled it down,' says the new man.

'Never miss a chance to go,' says Uncle Fred and goes off to the Gents.

It only takes five minutes to decide that this time it is not the police witness who is lying, but the bloke who says that he never went faster than fifty, and if he's a first-time speeder we will fine him the minimum and costs. If not, throw the book at him. We are clamping down on speeders. Offence of the month.

'All stand.'

He's a speeder all right. Got a record as long as your arm. Speeders don't bother me in the night. One for the policeman's personal file.

Mary Mallory sits beneath us, waiting for the call, 'Ma . . . ry Ma . . . ll . . . ory', to go echoing down the stairs. I've sussed the new man, it doesn't take long. One sitting and I know how he came to be a pillar of the community. A belt round the ear from his father. He is proud of his father . . . My father gave us all a good belt round the ear. That's how to deal with drunks in Paradise Street. They know what they're doing. Take the consequences. A good belt round the ear. If only I could think like that when the Mary Mallorys appear. That's it! A good belt round the ear. Short, sharp, shocks. Bring back the birch.

It sounds so good. Looks good in newspaper headlines, too. 'Local JP in Court Row – Bring Back Birch Call!' Hooray, say the readers. I could ask the new man what he will do when he gets a case of ear belting in his List . . . Informant – Police. Nature of Offence – Assault. We aren't fools – not all of us, anyhow – we read reports on recidivism. Short, sharp, shocks don't actually work. Look at the figures, but it sounds good. Short, sharp, shocks. We all know a permanent pay-packet would have a better influence. But you have to be a Friday Dove to say so out loud. They chuckle indulgently knowing that I can always be outvoted. Give her the key and she'd let them all out. You are not a Social Worker – you are a Magistrate. You are not a Counsellor – you are a Magistrate, here to administrate the Law. You are wearing a CND badge in Court. You are no good at this job.

Eleven forty-five. Most of the List is cleared. Drunks often come last. Gives them time to recover if it has been a blinder.

'That's the lot, Madam.'

'What about this Drunk charge?'

Ah!

Yes. The Clerk thinks it has been transferred to Court Number Nine.

Ah, Mary Mallory, I shall not sit in judgement upon you. There but for the grace of God and all that kind of thing.

'Like to retire for five minutes, Ma'am?' says the Clerk. He does not need to approach the Bench and murmur confidentially to me, it is nearly midday. The Public Gallery has gone back to its bedsits, or into the Library where it is nearly as warm as Number One Court. Not a Duty Solicitor to be seen, not in Court, anyway – Mario's Wine Bar? Twelve o'clock! See you.

'All stand.'

The Clerk and the Jailer stand and bow.

We exit. Wilson, Kepple and Betty.

'Never miss a chance to go,' says Uncle Fred.

'Smoke?' says the new man. They used to ask if it was all right.

In my capacity as Chairman I feel I should ask him something. Like where's your manners, Boy?

'How did you get on with your training?'

He says he is sorry it is over . . . only joking of course . . . and launches into a description of the hotel where they trained for a weekend. They did us proud. He says it over and over. Didn't get to bed till four in the morning.

'We did our training here,' I say. I dare say he thinks I'm talking about the golden age when coffee was served mid-morning.

'Ah, yes, they did us proud.'

Uncle Fred comes back with the Clerk who is full of explanation about the transferring and re-transferring of Mary Mallory.

'It was put into Number Nine, but their rape has gone on longer than they expected.'

I think they try out these lines on us. Like the one about two Porsches totalling £5.90, property of Debenhams.

'You could put that in the pantomime.'

'Not this year I'm afraid, Ma'am. Second busiest court in the country.'

I should not have opened my mouth when he said, That's about the lot, Ma'am. If I had not kept looking at the List I would not have blurted out, What about the drunk? and I would be queueing up for my subsidized omelette along with Uncle Fred.

The Clerk goes back to arrange for Mary Mallory to be brought up to Number One.

Wilson, Kepple and Betty go back. The Jailer bows. The Clerk bows. We bow.

'Call Mary Mallory.'

'Did you hear my belly rumble?' says Uncle Fred.

'Get it over quick,' says the new man.

Bloody cheek. This is *my* court! There is that one thing about being Chairman in court – no matter that they call you chair*man* – it is your court. You are the power and the glory. It's going to take a few years before the new man sits in Number One Court.

'Don't count on it!' Uncle Fred says it before I can get it

out. He's an old hand.

A policeman with an *aide-mémoire* comes into the Court.

You don't need to see what is going on down below. Rattle of keys. Clang of cell doors. Rattle of keys. Footsteps. Clatter along corridor. Up the steps. Jingle of keys. Mary Mallory appears in Number One Court.

The Clerk reads the charge.

'How do you plead?'

She does not answer but stares into the space ten inches or so before her eyes.

'Mrs Mallory?'

It takes time for her to adjust.

The policeman says, I swear by Almighty God that the evidence and so on and so on as though it were one word.

'May I refer to my notes, Sir? Madam – sorry Madam.'

Madam asks when they were made up as she is bound to, he replies as soon as possible after the incident as he is bound to.

'You should have left me there and I'd have been all right.'

Mary Mallory you haven't been all right for years. You smooth your dress. You are sobering up. You smooth back your hair. Christ, where am I? She looks at the Wardress . . . one of the old school, she makes my 40C-cup appear flat in comparison, not like the pert, shining WPCs with chests like gymnasts. Officially PCs because they purged The Force of sexism . . . The Wardress guides Mary Mallory through her paces. It is going all right. Uncle Fred and I usually agree about all the Mary Mallorys. A majority decision if the new man . . . it suddenly occurs to me that he must be the one who was on the carpet for making statements to the press about cleaning up the city. There are three types who are dedicated to cleaning up the city: women who long for the old days of hats, retired naval officers who have spent the greater part of their lives dirtying up cities on the other side of the world, and working-class blokes whose fathers belted them into a better class of society. Uncle Fred, let us dismiss . . . let her go . . . then I shall be able to digest my subsidized omelette and get to sleep tonight.

'Why didn't you leave me to sleep it off? I wasn't doing anybody any harm.'

There is an informal atmosphere in the huge, empty courtroom. I raise my eyebrows in query at the policeman. It is nearly one o'clock. Uncle Fred's stomach protests its emptiness – it expected a glass of beer at twelve o'clock. Everybody is hungry except Mary Mallory.

'We did at first, Ma'am, in Paradise Street. She seemed to be all right. I thought I would keep an eye on her.'

'What did you want to charge me for then?'

The policeman shrugs his shoulders.

'Next time I saw her, she had fallen down.' He pauses, knowing how it will sound. 'She went to sleep in the entrance of the Central Police Station.'

The day has come. I have gone along with things that were for the best, because if I didn't they might get somebody like the new man. Send some old bloke to prison for Christmas because that's the only place where anybody will keep him from sleeping rough, frozen to the ground in his own urine? Try the short, sharp shocks on kids from decrepit council estates because it's better than prison? Let millionaire drug pushers out on bail because they can afford Surrey houses and London barristers? I hear Mary Mallory pushing me off the fence where I have been sitting till my brain went numb.

'Is there anything you would like to tell the Court?' There is a long silence.

There always is when you ask any of the Mary Mallorys this question. How can you tell anything to a Court? Perhaps if we were in the little room behind the wood panelling. She's there to be Bound Over. My Kenny's only two, he kept on crying see, and we lives in married quarters. I never knew what was the matter with him, and when you're married to a sailor they an't never there – you got a fag love? ta – and when the kids keeps on and on grizzling and they says there an't nothing wrong you starts shouting at them. You'd think she'd a known, she got kids of her own, instead she comes round saying she'll knock the little bugger's head off if he don't stop grizzling. I said to her, you an't the only one who an't seen her husband for a year. She hit her neighbour, she doesn't deny it. Is there anything you would like to tell the Court?

'Have you any family?'
'Somewhere.'
'Do you work?'
'No.'
'What did you do . . . what was your job?'
'I used to be a nurse.'

That hurt . . . used to be.
She wants to say sod off what's it got to do with you but she's only at the beginning of her career as a woman without grace. When she's been down as long

as Barbara Charlesworth she will say it, or she will stand there bemused, her brain-cells picked off by anything remotely alcoholic, so stinking of her own body fluids and so pickled, that the new man will say I sometimes think Hitler had the right idea.

'Have you got any money?'
'Look,' she says, 'I'm an alcoholic, aren't I!'

It is her plea – she pleads Guilty/Not Guilty, her reason, her excuse. There is no more to be said. She knows, Uncle Fred knows, I know, we all know except the new man. There is nothing we can do. I know, I know. I must put her out of my mind. I must stop thinking I am a Social Worker. I am not a Counsellor. I must not get involved. If the rehabilitation centres are closed down, it is within the Law Of The Land to do so. I am here to administer the Law Of The Land.
And I'm sick to the stomach of it.
A sailor will buy her a double, perhaps she will pal up with another girl who will give her a shake-down for the night. Tomorrow . . . I'm an alcoholic, aren't I!

'You are down as No Permanent Address.'
'Yes.'
'Have you got somewhere to go?'
'No.'
'Have you any money at all?'
She smiles. 'After last night?'
Uncle Fred passes me a note. 'Give her a pound from funds and get her out of here. No costs.'
'Where will you go when you leave the Court?'
'I don't know, for God's sake. I'm an alcoholic, aren't I?'

Mary Mallory. Barbara Charlesworth. The verdict of the Court is that you shall henceforth be at the mercy of the New Man. The Wardress guides her back down to the Bridewell where she will be officially disposed of.
You got off light didn't you.
Wilson, Kepple and Betty do their exit.
Uncle Fred nips into the Gents.

New Man talks me through the echoing corridors of Justice, and to the Reserved for Magistrates Only car park.

A few lines. 'Dear Lord Chancellor . . .'
Inevitable really . . . this day.

New Man has gone. I turn the key in the ignition and the engine roars at the empty underground desolation.
My spirits rise.
A brief note. 'Dear Lord Chancellor . . .' and it will be over.

Off the Bench.
Off the Fence.
You got off light didn't you!

Taff at the kiosk says, you late today Luv. Working you overtime again are they. You want to come out on strike. We laugh, Taff still wears his 'Coal not Dole' sticker. I look for my Pass. It's all right Luv, I don't want to see it.

Taff doesn't want to see my Pass for the last time.
Above ground it is an ordinary January Friday.
'Dear Lord Chancellor, I have decided to . . . sod off!'

THE WRITER

THE WRITER

It was the sort of gathering where art has a capital A and the guests hurl superlatives. Shrill 'Darlings!' Starlings. Cocktails laid on – me, Visiting Author and Critic. Somebody asked what I thought of the new 'Credo'. Supposing this was yet another cult or dynamic arts magazine – 'Credo' being the kind of title in vogue at the time – I didn't respond with much interest.

'I've never heard of it,' I said.

The woman who had arranged the party (all that I knew of her was that her name was Gussie Goedere) pressed the red-tipped fingers of one hand to her breast.

'Not it, my dear Maria, he! Oh, and you've not read him. Imagine that! My dear, he is supreme!'

She raised her voice.

'Freddy, do come. Maria has never read Credo!'

He came.

'Freddy knows Credo – he's done him in tempera, haven't you darling?'

'Acrylic, actually,' he said.

'Well!' said Gussie Goedere. 'Just fancy, I'd have thought, a writer with your views, Maria . . . he's absolute genius! Our home-grown . . .'

Oh God! Another local genius. I'd had it up to here on

this last lecture tour with up and coming Steinbecks, Roy Campbells and Thomases of all kinds – R.S.s, D.M.s, and Dylans.

'. . . our Zulu Shakespeare.'

Of course – Shakespeare, who else!

Before she twirled off to another part of the room she instructed Freddy to brief me on this Credo.

It must have shown in my face.

'I know what you're thinking,' Freddy said, 'but don't be put off because he happens to be Gussie's Genius of the Month. Credo's good, but you must judge for yourself. Tell you what, I'll send you round something of his.'

I said, that'll be nice, and a couple of days later I received a nice little note and a book, which made Freddy unusual – he remembered a promise he'd made at a cocktail party. A hardback entitled *My People* – Credo Vuzamazulu Mutwa. I said it out loud, 'Credo Vuzamazulu Mutwa', more noticeable on a book cover than Maria Maugham.

I put the book into my suitcase with bits I had collected on this tour, and would probably not have given it a second thought had it not been that in the evening paper my attention was caught by the headline 'Threats to Life of Author!', and a photo of Credo Mutwa. An article said that the Zulu prophet and writer was in some danger because his latest book revealed tribal secrets.

Prophet! That was going some. Not just that, he was, according to the news item, a Zulu shangan, descended from the Great Shangan of Dingana. The accompanying photograph was, for security reasons, the report stated, the first ever published of him. It didn't explain why, now that his life had been threatened, it was all right to publish it.

Black Shakespeare or not, he's got a really good publicity agent hyping the book – Zulu/witchdoctor/

writer, and prophet too for goodness' sake, and with threats to his life, it couldn't fail. So, when I took my after-supper drink out on to the veranda I decided to have a look at the book.

In the blurb Credo was quoted as saying, 'If you think Africans are primitive, superstitious, riff-raff, try hurling a dead pig into a mosque and see what happens.' I liked that. I wanted to see what else he had to say.

It was a Saturday evening, and black workers in the gold mines were rehearsing their tribal dances for the tourist show next day. The sound of their drumming carried from the compound far out of the city. I don't know whether the sound of the drums helped create a mood, but before I reached the end of the first chapter I was immersed in a new experience of words – and I was delighted.

The Beginning

> There were no stars, no sun, moon or earth. Nothing existed but darkness itself – nothing existed but nothingness. It was a nothingness neither hot nor cold, dead nor alive – a nothingness frightening in its utter nothingness . . . there arose from it the great Mother Goddess.

The great Earth Mother with her quivering, four-breasted body, liquid fire flowing through her veins, breathing clouds of red-hot searing luminescence that could melt elephants. And the mate she longed for, a monstrous Tree of Life with its dozens of bloodshot eyes burning with lecherous hunger, scaly and studded with granite, diamonds and iron-ore.

Kei-Lei-Si who took her cyclopean child to the Kaa-U-La bird. And Az-Ha-Rrellel who owned metal beasts that crushed wild animals and made them into men.

I didn't know what to make of the book. Of course, not Shakespeare, but oh, lovely to read. Part history, part autobiography, part philosophy and a bit of politics.

I said some of the names aloud, mastering the new syllables, the new words, the Zulu names. I became absorbed in them, and when I had finished, the short night had gone and the dawn was coming pink in the sky.

Stretching out upon the bed I closed my eyes, but could not sleep for thinking about some of the things the author had written about himself. There had been a woman he was going to marry, but she was killed in the Sharpeville shootings. He wrote about riots in Rhodesia, apartheid, and retold the massacre of Dingana's women by Retief – yet said that he accepted the political fact of apartheid. I couldn't make the man out.

I wanted very much to see Mutwa before I went back to England. I knew that if I didn't see him now there wouldn't be another opportunity, because when my next novel was published it wasn't likely that I would be welcome in the country again.

I can't remember now what I had expected when I started reading. Because of Gussie's description 'black Shakespeare', possibly sonnets, or a kind of parallel *Hamlet* or *Lear*. How many good, new writers are blighted by being taken up by the Gussies. Credo Mutwa is Credo Mutwa and nobody else.

After that first reading, I really didn't care about his place in literature, but I did want to see the writer who had given me something new to think about – and I wanted to write again, for the first time in months.

I phoned Freddy to thank him, and mentioned that my interest had been aroused.

'Gussie said that you knew him . . . you painted him,

didn't you? Do you think you could arrange for me to meet him?'

He didn't answer immediately, then he said with an embarrassed laugh, 'This isn't England, you know.'

'I'm not with you,' I said.

'Sorry,' he said. 'Times like this I feel I have to apologize for our ridiculous laws. The fact that he's a writer doesn't mean that . . .' He stumbled on. 'It wouldn't be easy . . . you know what I mean? . . . Credo lives in township . . . You would have to get a permit.'

It was obvious he didn't want to become involved.

'Of course,' I said. 'I didn't think.'

I knew that he was making an excuse, he could have invited the writer to his studio, and I could have met him there.

'I'm sorry,' he said again.

'Ah well,' I said, 'it was just a thought.'

'You could apply for a permit. It would take about a week. Ah, but then you will have gone, won't you?'

'Yes, I shall be in Sweden in a week,' I said.

We politely said, 'Shame', so near, etcetera, etcetera, perhaps next time, and I thanked him again for the book. I should have realized that although starlings pose as free-thinking radicals, it's only talk.

Then I realized that perhaps I might be able to see the Zulu writer. The newspaper report mentioned that he worked in a curio shop – I could go there, and even if there was no chance of talking to him, I could possibly satisfy my curiosity.

I set off on the burning pavements of the city.

Johannesburg, like New York and many modern cities, is built to a boring but eminently logical plan, which is why I can't understand how I came to find myself in an area that was unmarked on my map.

Never mind, the novel that I was beginning to work out would have to be set in such streets as I found myself in. An allegory. The legend of the Earth Mother's desire for a mate and how he came to her, the terrible Tree of Life studded with granite, diamonds and iron-ore. The story of black African women pursued relentlessly by manufacturers and image-makers to become mere outlets for commodities like Western women.

I wandered about, no longer trying to find my way back to the street where I would find Credo Mutwa in his curio shop. My instincts had led me to this part of the city. Here were the characters I would need.

My sandals became covered by red dust; a not-quite unpleasant smell of rotting fruit pervaded the thick air. I looked into the dim interiors of rackety shops with black-looking carcases of meat; a store crammed with bolts of bright cloth, vivid sweets, pots, pans and cheap jewellery; another where, behind a cracked and fly-blown window, were displayed jars of bright powder, seeds, herbs and the mummified body of a monkey-like creature.

Squatting women, some with babies slung in shawls, sorted coloured beads and dried melon-seeds making necklaces for tourists; a light-coloured man ordered about a few young African boys who were dismantling clapped-out old bikes; a little group of excited men rattled dice and threw them down with panache.

I had looked into the black shiny faces of the squatting women, the bicycle scavengers, roasted corn vendors, messenger and delivery boys, and thought I saw their tribal past as Credo Mutwa had written of it, that time when the Zulu danced and pounded the dry soil of the veldt to red dust – and I was sure that I knew them.

It was like a morning spent writing, I felt I had been brushing shoulders with my characters in a world of my own creation. I decided that when I met Credo I would tell him my idea for the new novel, speaking with him would crystallize the mass of atoms of ideas.

I don't know what got into me that day. My imagination led me into the future, lecture notes gathered in my head . . . 'The Art of Credo Mutwa' . . . the American college circuit . . . what a dramatic opening to a lecture . . . Mutwa appearing on the podium, feathered head-dress . . . enormous possibilities.

Eventually I found the curio shop and suddenly became nervous. In my tours lecturing and promoting my books, I have met a premier, two prime ministers, a head of state and two winners of Nobel prizes for literature – yet I felt apprehensive at the thought of meeting this obscure Zulu writer.

Near the shop was a large concrete container of shrubs and canna lilies, and I sat pretending to look at them, but in reality trying to see inside the place where the writer worked. The picture that had appeared in the newspaper had shown a light-brown young man with plump arms, draped in a lynx-skin, and posed 'throwing the bones', while the dust-jacket of his book showed him sitting amid witch-doctor accoutrements, resplendent in the high feathered head-dress, collars and beads of a shangan.

He had an intelligent face and looked proud and splendid, and I had a momentary vision of him looking down his noble nose at this five-foot-tall, plump English-woman whose novels he had probably never heard of.

A black man came out of the shop. I watched as he mopped water over the window and squeezed it off. He had left the shop door open, making it easier for me to make up my mind to go in.

The traffic was heavy while I waited to cross the road to the curio shop. As I started to cross, a car hooted. The cleaner looked at me as I jumped back on to the pavement. The incident was over in two seconds. One second in which I recognized the 'boy', and one to realize that I was no different from Gussie when it came to Credo Vuzamazulu Mutwa – no, that's not exactly right, I did have the sense to take the notes I had made that morning, and thrust them into the nearest litter bin.

THE SNOW FOX

THE SNOW FOX

I was eighty-three yesterday. Not that I look it, so everybody says, and I still love to get myself up properly when I go out.

Our lads – lads! they're all a piece above fifty – well, they booked up to take me out to dinner. I like the kind of restaurants they go to now they've got to be directors and managers and the like. Places where they set fire to steaks and nobody pays with money. It's a chance to dress up, have a peach rinse, wear dangly earrings, high-heels – not as high as at one time, but high enough. I don't like to look like an old woman.

Anyway, we were ready to go when Peggy says, 'Hold on a minute', and she went off upstairs and came down carrying a fur stole.

'It's mink,' she said. 'More your style than mine. Here, put it on.'

'Eh, it's absolutely beautiful,' I said. And as I said it and felt the fur against my face, I was back sixty-odd years looking in the window of Moxon's Emporium.

Them days – for girls anyroad – soon as you left school it were service or one of the mills. I'd heard enough about service from my mother, so I went as a runner-on at the knitwear factory. I'd have loved to go on at school or work in the Post Office but . . . ah well, there you are. Nobody liked mill-work, not really, and after we had finished our shift, we used to burst out of the mill-gates and try to reach the end of the jitty before the hooter stopped. It was daft, but we weren't supposed to leave us benches until the hooter had gone, so getting to the end of the jitty like that felt like putting one over on them.

The jitty came out in the Market Place and we used to slow down and have a shop-window randy before we went home to us tea. Eight or ten girls flaunting around, making out we didn't care about the lads calling and whistling. That was the time when Moxon's was new. It was a big attraction. They had this window-dresser who went in for displays that would knock your eye out.

This day I'm telling you about, we got to Moxon's and the centre window, the big one by the revolving door, had been all done out in black satin background, and mounds of fake snow all sprinkled with glitter and laying on this snow, with its tail curled round so as it looked like real, was this beautiful animal. It was white, with blue glass eyes and a great fluffy tail. I tell you, I'd never seen owt like it. There wasn't any price on it, Moxon's was too posh for that, there was just this card with copper-plate letters saying 'Exclusive – Snow Fox'.

'Eh, that's absolutely beautiful!' I said.

Rose, that's my sister, you know, the one that died a year or two back, said, 'You know who'll buy that, don't you?'

'Aye, Mrs Tibbett,' one of the girls said. And everybody said of course she would, because Henry Tibbett was a buttie at the pit and butties' wives always dressed like ladies, and Henry Tibbett's wife reckoned to be best dressed of the lot.

'She'll not,' I said. 'I shall.'

Well they all laughed, they knew how I was about clothes and getting all dolled up. Sometimes, when we were having us break, somebody would say, 'Hey, Jess, tell us what you'd get if you had a hundred pound.' And I would let my fancy fly. Oh, I knew what I'd buy; dance-dresses with bugle beads, a cloak with silk lining, French shoes and gloves with little pearl buttons right up to the elbow – so, of course, when I said I would have the snow fox, they thought it was a bit more of my romancing.

But it were not. I looked at it and I knew I must have it. White fur like that didn't go with a neck of some old woman like Henry Tibbett's wife – why she must have been getting on forty – it belonged round a young neck like mine.

I was eighteen, I couldn't have been older because I was still living at home and working at the knitwear mill. All of us girls used to do running-on, it was the sort of work we did better than anybody, we had quick fingers. They still do it, it's a skilled job, they didn't pay much, but we didn't do too bad on piece-work.

I made above fifteen shilling a week. When our Rose and me tipped up our wages on a Friday, my mother always left us something for ourselves. She took out enough for us board and left us about five shilling apiece for ourselves – that's twenty-five pence in this new money, but it was worth a lot more then.

When we were working we use to gossip. A lot about lads – some of the girls were courting, but not me. I couldn't understand them always wanting to be with the same one. All I wanted was a good-looking smart arm to parade about on when I was in my finery. To be honest, I don't think I gave a thought to anything except clothes. Not the sort of clothes, though, mill-girls usually wore, but fashion, class. Flouncy dresses and hats that made people look twice.

I can hear our Rose now. 'Eh, our Jess, you're never going to buy that? Why they've got same thing up at Stores a quarter the price.' But she didn't understand. No amount of telling her would make her see the difference between the style and finish of what I wanted, and what they sold at Stores – Co-op like, as they say down your way.

It wasn't only our Rose, all the girls were like that, always thinking how cheap you could get something for, or how long it would last. Well, you can understand, I suppose, if you think about it we didn't have a lot of money. But to me that seemed all the more reason to spend what you did have on something worth having. So when any of them rolled their eyes at a little bit of a hat that had cost four-and-elevenpence . . . that were a week's money, so that'll tell you . . . well, I used to say 'Why not? I've worked for it!' I know they thought I was daft with my money, but they saw it was fair enough if that's what I wanted.

Ah, but I tell you, my father didn't think it was fair enough. There was always trouble. Every time I bought something there was a row. As soon as I got through the door with a bag, he'd draw his eyebrows together and wouldn't he glower at the bag, why you'd think whatever was in it would shrivel up or bust into flames.

'There'll come a day when you'll need that money,' he'd say, 'but don't come crawling to me, because you'll find none here.'

I wasn't afraid of him, he'd have liked me to be, but I wasn't.

'You needn't to worry,' I'd say, 'I'd do owt before I'd crawl to you or any man!' And I meant it. And I haven't changed! I'd stand there not giving an inch and see bitterness take over his face. I began to hate coming home when he was there even when I hadn't been spending. That's a terrible thing to say about your own father – but it's true.

Looking back I can understand why he said I was a fool with my money. He worked at the pit, not on the coal face where the good money was, but in the engine sheds. I never found out how he came to be doing that because he came from a well-off family – they owned quite a big shop in Nottingham – so he must have been brought up with things a lot better than they were in our house. But he didn't have to be bitter.

D'you know, I've never thought about this before . . . he used to be a radio fanatic – always had house full of men, the whole place was strung up with wires, and there was these jars full of acid that used to be something to do with it, oh yes was quite the high sarrag about radios then . . . what I was thinking about – it must have cost quite a bit to buy all that stuff when you think about it – nobody else had anything like it as I know of – oh yes, he was the big I Am there. I'm just wondering . . . perhaps he thought he was going to be God's gift to radio but couldn't afford it – he was like that – thought good things were wasted on the 'igh palloi.

He thought women should be submissive, which my mother was. And he was a bully because when I stood up to him he would always turn on her saying that she encouraged me – but she didn't . . . didn't dare! So in the end I stopped standing up to him. I wasn't going to let him stop me, though, but it made me underhand and secretive. It isn't in my nature to be like that, it never was. It took a lot of the pleasure out of buying something new.

I was only young when I first started earning. In them days, if you were clever at school, you could go in for a test and if you passed you could leave, aye, and go to work in a factory – just think about that – and it always seemed it was the girls that passed – isn't that terrible? . . . anyway I used to run home with anything new I'd bought, even the sound of the bag crackling would make it exciting. And we had hat-boxes then – but it was later I started buying hats – you can't imagine the thrill it was taking off the ribbon and going down into all the tissue-paper. First, when he started his carping, I used to take things straight upstairs and not bring them out until he had gone out. But after a bit he'd only got to see me with a bag to start a row.

But I was still determined he wasn't going to domineer me. To keep the peace I never brought owt into the house, I used to sling it all into the back of the coal-shed until he was out of the way, or put things on in the toilet which was next to the coal-shed and sometimes change back later on.

When I think about it, it's a marvel what I used to do with five or six shilling a week. There were no credit cards like there are now. There were clothing clubs and tally-men . . . I haven't heard of a tally-man for years, I wonder if they're still about . . . if it weren't for the clubs and the tally-man I don't know how most folks would have got on.

Then there were a bit up-class people like Mrs Pickup.

Now, she kept a little shop, what you'd call a boutique now, where you could get really nice things and pay them off weekly. It weren't a deal different from the clubs really, except for the kind of things she sold. Pretty things. Fashionable and not meant to last, they did though, they were real quality. Nearly all my money went to Mrs Pickup . . . well at least until that day as I'm telling you when I saw this here snow fox.

Up till then I had never bought anything at Moxon's, and when I said I was going to have the fur, I didn't think how I was going to pay. Everything I ever had was on the never-never. And I'd never thought about how much it would cost. You could get a red fox with two tails for one pound ten (a pound fifty like), well you don't want to ask – I nearly dropped through the floor – this white one was five pound. Well, it was a fortune.

Moxon's was so high-class it never occurred to me they'd have anything to do with never-never . . . well I tell you, that was an eye-opener. The assistant would ask you straight out, 'Cash or account, madam?' The butties' wives and managers' and stockingers' wives, they all did it. I was really shocked when I found out . . . working-class people hated not being able to pay cash down, we were ashamed of it, yet everybody had to do it . . . and that was what shocked me at first, Henry Tibbett's wife and that lot, with all their money weren't a bit embarrassed at not paying cash. The only difference between the clothing club and Moxon's is that they called it having an account – aye and they didn't charge as much interest at Moxon's.

I don't know whether it was because I went in dressed up, but they just asked me straight out when I went in to price the fur, 'Would you like to open an account?' Not a bit furtive, not at all, just straight out, 'Would you like to open an account?' And I came home with the snow fox and some pretty new shoes and a hat – and I could have had a date with the under-manager. Ha, but I didn't want to spoil it, him finding out I worked at the mill . . . well, I reckon I must have found a gold mine of really nice things there. It meant working some extra time, but it was worth it.

I can remember it as though it was yesterday. Going home with all my bags and boxes and knowing that my father had gone down to London on some union jaunt, so I could go straight into the house and show my Mam and our Rose.

'Eh, our Jess, I don't know how you dare,' our Rose said. 'Fancy getting white! There'll be soots on it as soon as you set foot outside the house.' And she went on about how was I going to get it cleaned – our Rose was always practical like that, I hadn't given a thought to owt like that. But my Mam, you should have seen the look on her face. I can just see her, brushing her hand down the whole pelt, trying out the jaw of the fox that was the fastening clip, and polishing the eyes with her apron. And when I was all dressed up she said, 'Well, our Jess, it's fair beautiful. I always knew you were cut out to be a lady.'

Can you imagine what I felt like going out that evening? I could walk out of our house dressed to kill and come back again knowing that my father was two hundred miles away. And I was meeting a soldier down town, one as always got turned out immaculate.

When I got home that evening there was just my Mam and me having a cup of cocoa, she suddenly went to the dresser and fetched out a photograph . . . a big one, they used to be called cabinets. She didn't say anything but just opened up the cover. I couldn't really believe it – it was me, yet it wasn't quite, yet it was so much like me. My face, hair in the same curly fringe, my way of holding my head when I know I'm being looked at, and my same smile. She had on three ropes of pearls and her shoulders were bare except for a fur draped round them – a snow fox just exactly like mine.

'I just thought I'd show you,' my Mam said. 'Don't tell your father or there'll be hell to pay. It's been in the attic twenty year or more. I just thought I'd show you.'

'Who is she?'

I could tell she felt she'd already gone too far. She started to take the photo back upstairs.

'It's all in the past,' she said.

'Mam, you can't not tell me now. She could be my twin, couldn't she?'

She didn't say anything for a bit, then all she said was, 'She was your father's twin, and it's no good asking me anything else because I don't know, and if you ever ask him he'll know it was me as showed you.'

I don't know if it was because I looked so much like her and knowing that he had cut her out of his life . . . and ours too, she were me auntie . . . but I made up my mind I wasn't going to put up any longer with the way he treated me.

He came back from London full of it, he actually sat in the kitchen telling us about the petition they'd gone down to London with. He seemed a different man . . . if only he could have always been like that, but when he was at the pit he hardly said a word. I had already decided I was going to stop that hole-in-the-corner business of getting ready to go out, and with him being so pleasant to everybody, it seemed like a good omen.

When I came downstairs ready, he and Mam and our Rose were sitting at the table drinking tea. He was reading out the petition to them. He looked up and saw me . . . It still gives me the horrors thinking about it. It was like a devil in him. He didn't move a muscle, but it seemed like he was hitting me, beating me. I couldn't repeat the terrible things he said, nor couldn't I believe he could think such things about me. What it amounted to was, he said I had been going with men – you know what I mean – he said the only way a mill-girl could dress up like that was if she was doing something dirty . . . I shall remember his words to my dying day: 'Strutting about the town like a bloody whore, dripping in white furs and pearls.'

Well, I wasn't wearing pearls and never had, so I knew

then that it wasn't only me he was talking about, perhaps it wasn't me at all. I dare say it was why he was always so bitter with me . . . but that didn't make it any easier looking at his hate and listening to his bitterness.

My Mam and our Rose looked terrified, and it came to me calm and clear that while I was there I was making everybody's life a misery, and it would only get worse. Aye, and my Mam were such a gentle, nice person . . . I wish you could have met her. Anyroad, I just turned my back on him and went upstairs and changed into some everyday clothes. Then I took out every bit of my finery from the places where it was hidden and put everything in a big box, and put my bits and pieces of working things in a case.

I went back downstairs, they were all sitting like gravestones. My father didn't move. I had all my payment cards from Mrs Pickup, going right back, and Moxon's account payments, and I laid them out in front of him like a game of patience and on top I put all my overtime chitties. He didn't move an inch. Then I went.

He was sitting facing the yard window, so I knew he could see me. I put my box of lovely things on the stones, fetched the paraffin can and poured it over and set a match to it.

I used to see my sister at work, and my Mam would come to my lodgings when he was gone to the pit. Sometimes I would see him in the street, but he never looked at me even if we came face to face. Over the years he grew to look more and more bitter-looking, and I could have cried for him. Soon after I left, our Rose married and went away down South. He had twelve grandchildren and never spoke a word to one of them, and my Mam was an old woman at forty-five.

I thought about all this yesterday. Our lads, and their

wives and most of the grandchildren, a great table full of us, having shrimp cocktails and bits of things on swords at that posh restaurant, but it weren't the place, it was us, still sticking together. I know everybody don't get on . . . it'd be a queer family if they did, but I've always said blood's thicker than water. It's like being part of a long story, a saga, all the ups and downs, the young ones just starting, not knowing, and me being part of it.

And I thought about him and I thought what a fool he had been denying himself all that.

Anyway, I thought I would tell somebody. They've always been on at me to write things down, and I've always been meaning to and now you've bought me this smashing little tape-recorder for my birthday I'll be talking to you quite a lot.

THE MELON-SEED GIRL

THE MELON-SEED GIRL

I have often wondered how a beggar claims a lucrative stand. Is there some kind of agreement, franchise or concession on the begging patches outside the big stores in Johannesburg? The taking of these positions isn't casual, in fact the beggars appear to be organized and keep regular hours. They are always black. There are white beggars, called Poor Whites, but they are a furtive lot, some haunting hotel entrances with thin stories about having lost a wallet, or being mugged by the tsotsis, others waylaying travellers on isolated roads, blocking the way with clapped-out old vans. Latter-day highwaymen.

We lived for a time in Rosebank, which is in the modern, leafy suburbs, the shopping area is all jacaranda trees and fountains and modern sculpture. Not an area where one found Poor Whites – perhaps there were unwritten apartheid rules – anyway, for whatever reason, all the Rosebank beggars were black.

There were three main department stores, in two of which one was never served by anyone with an Afrikaans accent, but by a very superior English-type assistant modelled upon what was supposed to be pre-war Bond Street, but just missing it. The third store was cheap and cheerful, blatant and vulgarly intrusive on the rest of the tasteful scene. It announced itself in huge letters 'OK STORES'.

The patch at the front of the OK was worked by a legless beggar of about thirty-five. He was broad-shouldered and very handsome, with high cheekbones and good teeth. I never went into the OK but he was there, seated on a four-wheeled trolley like Porgy, with a few cronies playing dice and sharing cigarettes.

The patch at the back of the OK, by the carpark, was worked by a small girl. At a guess she was about eight years old. Thin, bony and always dressed in the same cheap cotton shift and woollen beret. Everyone who used the store received a grin from her as she held out an armful of necklaces. You can get these necklaces anywhere now, but then you had actually to go to Africa to buy the delicate, warm, brown melon-seeds made up into long strings of flower-motifs. I often wore them, they didn't last long because the thread holding the seeds together was cheap – built-in obsolescence.

For the first twenty years of my life, I had that kind of English working-class upbringing where you are taught to look upon tips and hand-outs as degrading, at the same time as learning to share and share alike. Consequently, I had no idea how to behave towards maimed beggars, or the old ones who stood in doorways holding out shrivelled hands and making frail noises. The English working-class philosophy didn't work here where there were large numbers of beggars.

Sometimes I filled my purse with coins and gave to all and sundry. Other times I went out of my way to avoid them. Whatever I did I always ended up feeling guilty. It wasn't quite the same with the melon-seed girl. Whenever I went to the OK she would grin and hold out her necklaces. I would smile and give her ten cents. She sold necklaces and I bought them. A straightforward deal. I had dozens of the things.

Living with us at the time was Sara, a Swazi. In the more usual order of South African society ours should have been a servant/mistress relationship, but she wasn't cut out to serve, nor I to be served. We were thrown together by the company who could arrange lifestyles at a distance of thousands of miles. The flat was serviced which meant that Sara and I had nothing to do all day except prepare an evening meal, so we spent hours and days talking about our families, about how different and how similar life was in our respective homelands.

She had been living in Johannesburg since she was about fourteen and was proud of the fact that no one could put one over on her so, although she was the younger, she took me in hand when she found out that I was a mere country-girl, and English at that. She taught me to watch for the butcher who weighed his fingers along with the steak, and which was a 'going-to-Portygee' and a 'not-going-to-Portygee' greengrocer, how to get to the library without running the gauntlet of the alcoholics, and other essential knowledge of city life.

The first few necklaces she let pass, indicating her disapproval only by a pursing of her lips, but then one day she thought things had gone far enough.

'You have been to the OK beggar.'

It wasn't a question, nor yet quite an accusation, more a statement of fact that needed to be discussed. I felt caught out and began to make excuses, which shows something of the kind of relationship we had.

'Well, I thought I would send them home to my mother.'

Sara and my mother were on pretty good terms. They wrote to one another. I never found out what they wrote about, but I sometimes heard my mother's phrases in Sara's mouth: 'You should be more careful! . . . Don't let them get away with that! . . . Don't go out without shoes.'

She opened the discussion.

'These sort of rubbish is no good for The Mother.' The Mother was a kind of title Sara had given my mother. 'The Mother like nice thing.'

'They are nice.'

No accounting for taste! She didn't say it with words – just the eyes.

I should have shut up, but blundered on.

'Well, it's really that little girl at the OK. I can't pass her.'

'Why not?'

'She expects me to stop. She'd be disappointed.'

'So?'

'She's so little.'

Sara blew away my explanation.

'And she looks so thin.'

'Well, you buying these thing don't do her no good. She sells these rubbish just only for her father to buy his whisky.'

'How d'you know that?' I need not have asked. Sara knew!

'Everybody know!' she said. 'He always have sit at OK with the whisky in his cart.'

'Who? The one without the legs?'

'Yes, he.'

'Is he her father?'

'Of course. She sells beads to get his whisky.'

There was no more to be said. Sara was teetotal, whisky did the Devil's work. Everybody know!

Now it was out in the open – her disapproval of my melon-seed deals.

Sara was my best and only friend in that city, so from then on, not wanting to upset her, I was more discreet.

When winter comes to the South African veldt, it comes with bright sunshine, clear blue skies and bitter, bitter winds that feel as though they have been sucked up on the Russian steppes then expelled down the skyscraper canyons of Johannesburg. So, when the May winds started, I stopped my meandering round the Rosebank piazzas and went instead to the city centre.

I didn't see the melon-seed girl or her Porgy father for about two months, until one Saturday morning. There was an exhibition of tropical fish in a store in Rosebank, so while John took the children to see the fish, I went to have a look round the shops. It was a freezing morning and I was wrapped in a furry coat. I got right up to the door of the OK before I saw her, but there she was, just as when I had last seen her back in March when the days were still warm. She was still in her cotton shift, standing with one foot tucked up into her thigh. No, not just as she had been, only superficially so. Her brown skin had gone grey, and instead of eagerly looking about for customers, she stood with shoulders hunched. As soon as she saw me her face split into a grin. My warm coat shamed me into fatuity as I caught hold of her hand.

'You are so cold,' I said.

Instead of telling me of course anybody would be in that wind, with no shoes and a thin dress, she smiled straight into my eyes. In any B movie of the thirties, the woman would have draped her warm coat round the girl's bony shoulders and the problems of black Africa would have been solved.

I pointed to the necklaces.

'How many?'

'Ten cent.'

'How many to sell?'

She shrugged.

I took a necklace and held up a thumb.

'One?'

She nodded.

I took another and held up a finger.

'Two?'

I continued taking necklaces and counting until I held her whole stock.

'Twenty-five. Yes?'

She nodded. 'Yes.'

'Each for ten cents?'

Another nod.

'Two rand and fifty cents. Yes?'

'Yes,' she agreed.

I gave her the money and told her, 'Now go.'

She went, giving me a waggling-finger wave as she disappeared into the warmth of the OK store.

I thrust the necklaces under my shopping. Twenty-five. Most of the things in the bag I had got for Sara who would be waiting at the top of the stairs to take them from me when I got home. I might have dumped the necklaces, but couldn't bring myself to do it, all the effort that had gone into their making – the old working-class upbringing again. I put the problem aside and went into a coffee-bar where I had arranged to meet John and the children.

When he came in John had his My God! expression on. It usually meant that he had had a brush with the system.

'Dad bought hundreds . . .'

'Drink your Coke!'

The elder of our two knew when to shut up, but not the other one.

'But you did, Dad. Lots of beads. Hundreds.'

John plunged both hands into his overcoat pockets and pulled out a tangled mass of melon-seed necklaces.

'Well, there was this little kid – blue with cold – out the back of the OK. Nothing on her feet . . .'

I expect my expression halted him. I pulled out my bundle of necklaces.

The children didn't know what to make of our laughter.

On our way back to the car we told the children not to tell Sara about the necklaces which we would leave in the boot of the car.

As we rounded the corner there she was.

Her eyes swivelled from John to me and back again. Then she gave out with her grin.

When I stopped and put down my bag she looked perplexed, but continued standing with her foot tucked up. I tipped out the tangle of necklaces on to the pavement. She looked mildly curious but, no doubt, she had seen it all from her place at the OK. Never surprised at anything people like me did. I had carte blanche. Hot water sprang from taps inside my house. My bathroom was quite likely as large as her family's living room. A policeman would take my word against hers. I used the 'Blanke toilette', she used the 'Swart'.

Untangling the necklaces, I hung them separately about her neck. One or two people halted their stride momentarily, wondering what was going on. She watched carefully. When I had finished, I gave her the same sort of waggle of fingers that she had given me earlier and went off into the carpark.

From that morning on the nature of our deals changed. I would give her ten cents – she would hand me a necklace – I would slip it over her head. The other beggars remained. The child was still exploited by her father. Her father was still a handsome man without legs. The frail hands still appeared from doorways. And the only one of them I could ever look in the eye was the child – but don't ask me why.

COMMEMORATIVE STONES

COMMEMORATIVE STONES

'Sixth June, nineteen hundred and forty-four.'

Anna reads aloud the date on the memorial stone. An open-shore breeze blows from Portsmouth Harbour, twirling the drapes of her sari about her legs. She has not worn such a dress for almost forty years. Not since 6 June 1944 – D-Day, and she has worn it today only to please her granddaughter, Shalina.

Anna brought some fine silk from Delhi as a gift for her granddaughter, and Shalina, so pleased at the novelty of being dressed in it, insisted that they walk out together in the traditional dress of their ancestors.

Sixth June, nineteen hundred and forty-four.

The year I was eighteen. Still living with Father and Mother in Newtown. Newtown, Barkampur.

There was a war going on. Evidence of it was everywhere. Young British soldiers and airmen thronged the bazaars in tropical uniform as stiff as beetle cases.

'Why have they come here?' I asked Father.

'Anna!' The mock despair and disappointment. 'Why?' The theatrical incredulity. 'You ask "Why?", when India is part of our empire. You, the grandchild of an Englishman from Portsmouth, a man from the same city as

Lord Nelson? What have you been doing in school for all these years, haven't they taught you history?'

'Is this all there is?' Anna asks, holding the silk in place.

'Yes, Grandma,' says Shalina.

'It is not very big. I thought it would have been a much grander thing altogether.'

Shalina looks surprised. The litter-strewn, scruffy little garden with its lump of stone has always been there. A short-cut to the beach and the pier.

'Grandpa wasn't anything to do with D-Day, was he?'

'Goodness, no. I was not even then married.'

'Why did you want to see it, then?'

Anna gazes at the rough surface of the stone as if to find the answer there. Perhaps because the date was imprinted upon her memory as deeply as upon the stone.

When the news of the D-Day landings had reached Barkampur, I was sitting on the veranda to get away from Father's continual expounding of battle strategy. I was quite unaware that daylight had gone. I remember stirring the air about my face with a straw fan. For half an hour I succeeded in switching off my mind. I tried to imagine what a night in England must be like. Was it ever like this?

Father was for ever talking about England, but always about its history: kings and queens, great industries, laws and customs, always leading in the end to the forefathers, the Portsmouth Fletchers. He never talked about its streets or flowers, its markets, its customs. But then Father had never been to that country he claimed as his own. It was from Gordon I had learned what little I knew then about England.

'Ah, you'd love it,' he said. 'Everything's green. Not like here, not dusty and hard-baked. Our rivers have got real water in them – not the stuff you've got.' In those days the river was a yellow slug at the end of the dry season. Perhaps it still is.

How indignant I had felt.

'It is not now at its best. There has been practically no rain for quite some time, in fact it is quite overdue. You must see our river after the rains, it then runs fast. Also it is much wider then.'

'Ah, I love the funny way you speak,' he had said. Until then I had not known that anybody thought the way I spoke was funny. Of course, I was aware that my accent was different from the whites, the government officials and people like that, but not funny. They spoke with a 'yaw-yaw' jaw. It was different, too, from Indians who spoke English in a variety of rhythms and stresses.

I asked Father, 'How did we come to get our accent?'

'Accent? Accent? Who has said that we have any accent? It is the purest of English.' And when I had mentioned Gordon, he had become irritated.

'It must be that your young man, because he comes from the north of England, does not recognize the Hampshire accent that our family has retained. It is our heritage, the legacy of my father, your grandfather Fletcher.'

I started listening closely to the way the British servicemen spoke. Such a variety of pronunciation, but none at all like my own and the rest of the mixed-race population of Barkampur.

Quarter-master sergeant Gordon Bradley. He had been one of many young airforce men that Mother and Father had invited into our home. They were hospitable people, but I remember how embarrassed I felt upon overhearing Father telling Mother, 'Anna will meet an altogether entirely superior type of young man.'

Mother had agreed. 'Altogether superior.'

Gordon was on a more permanent posting in India than most of the young men who visited our bungalow on Sunday afternoons, and gradually we drifted into the position where he was thought of as 'Anna's young airman'.

'Grandma?' Shalina, holding down her fluttering skirts, stands patiently.

'Goodness, child. I was miles away. You must be bored, but I should like to stop here just a few minutes longer. Why don't you go and fetch us some ice-cream or some sweets.'

Shalina, pleased to experiment again with the novelty of wearing the sari, walks off to the pier.

Anna seats herself on a wooden bench. A bit disturbed, but not able to put her finger on why. She has not much idea of the D-Day expedition, except vaguely as some good item of news on that evening almost forty years ago. She wonders why she does not want to break the mood, but to remember 6 June 1944 in this unattractive corner of the south coast of England, thousands of miles from home.

She closes her eyes, and the sound of waves on the shingle beach becomes the sound of mortar and pestle, and she remembers an aroma of cumin and pepper and Grandmother Amina preparing food in her tiny kitchen.

After Grandfather Fletcher had died, Father had paid to have an extension made to our bungalow and Grandmother Amina came to live there with quiet dignity. She dressed, cooked and lived as any Kumar, Chandhuri or Singh grandmother, but she was Mrs Fletcher who lived in the 'granny-annexe' of her pale-skinned son's home, my father's home, my home. A central figure in the Fletcher history, part of it, yet not really belonging.

Father's attitude to Grandmother Amina was a mixture of pride, affection, and something else he was probably unaware of – he always felt that he had to explain her.

'She is the woman my father gave up his own country to marry. He loved her more than England.'

I grew up with a romantic image of Grandfather. Self-imposed exile because of his passion for Amina Battacharia.

Sixth June, nineteen hundred and forty-four. Yes, that was the date that divided her life, the date on the lump of stone.

'Why did you want to see it?' young Shalina had asked.

Suddenly she knows why.

It was the day I found out who I am.

I had been lighting the hanging kerosene lamp on the veranda when Father had appeared at the door.

'We have landed! It will not be very long now.'

Father had an Indian mother, was brought up in Barkampur and, although an official on the Indian railway, he had never travelled further than the hundred or so miles to Gupkar, yet he always spoke of the British forces as 'we'.

'It won't be long now, you just see.'

He went back indoors, leaving me to think. No more putting it off, I had to make up my mind.

Grandmother Amina was preparing her evening meal and, as she worked, there was a swish of silk and a jingle of bangles and earrings. I remember going to her end of the bungalow, and Grandmother looked up, pleased.

'Have you come to eat with me?'

'Not tonight. Perhaps tomorrow.'

We sat together. Our silence was easy, relaxed. Then

Grandmother asked, 'What will you tell the young man?'

'What is for me to tell?'

'Do you think because I am a thousand years old that I do not remember how a young man looks when he wants a certain woman?'

The silver and fire-opal drops in Grandmother's ears tinkled and gleamed as she nodded and ground seeds and pods. I waited for her to continue but she said nothing.

'What do you think I should do?'

'It is clear that the British airman wants you. The question being, does he want in marriage? And if in marriage, then each must ask in which country is this marriage to become established?'

I followed Grandmother's movements as she dripped oil into a pan, then replied, 'The question does not arise as to any choice of country. Gordon is not in the airforce just for the war, he will soon become an officer. There is no question of staying here.'

'What does my son say?'

'I have not told Father that Gordon has proposed marriage, but you know what he would say.'

She gave me a wry smile.

'He would say that it is impossible that you should not go to England. Home of Fletchers.'

We were both quiet for a few minutes while onions sizzled, then I got up to leave.

'I must go. Gordon will soon be coming to collect me. I must give him an answer tonight. He has been patient.'

Grandmother nodded, the girasol stones gleamed. 'Come tomorrow. I will cook for you also.'

In the sea-front rock-garden, Anna looks about for Shalina, and glimpses the flutter of the blue sari as she feeds coins into a fruit machine on the pier. 'I wasn't much older than her in 1944.' Suddenly Anna wants the visit to the D-Day memorial to finish, she wishes Shalina would come.

The next evening I went to eat with Grandmother. A meal with her was always a little celebration, a ceremony. She placed the dish between us, and when we were eating said, 'Would you like to tell me?'

'You know already. You cannot fail to have heard Father through the wall. He shouted. He was angry.'

'Because voices come through walls, does not mean that I listen. If there is something to tell, I would like to hear it from the one who is telling.'

'Gordon wishes that we should marry. To be married in England.'

Grandmother nodded. 'My son has always wished for such a thing.'

'Yes, it is what he wishes.'

I realized that I had been stirring the rice about on my plate not speaking. Grandmother did not approve of such behaviour, but she was an understanding old lady.

'Grandmother,' I asked, 'why did you not go to England with Grandfather? From the time when I was very little it seemed that he talked only of England. Why did he stay in India?'

'He stayed here for me.'

'Because you wanted to remain here?'

'Not at all. I would have gone anywhere he asked.'

'Then why choose India?'

'Your grandfather said it was to protect me.'

'From what?'

'From people who think it a first-class thing to have white skin, and second-class to have brown skin, and very bad for first-class and second-class to come together.'

I thought that Grandmother had very likely never before spoken in this open way except to Grandfather. For, apart from her natural reticence, to whom could she have spoken?

'But there are people like that also in this country, would it be different in England?'

'In England there are not so many such marriages, I believe. Here there are more. Here children of such unions have a place. Areas such as Newtown.'

Suddenly I felt very mature, seeing what no one else seemed ever to have done. Poor Grandmother! Disowned by her own princely father, and cut off from her family and traditions, she had come to live in Newtown, the mixed-race area of Barkampur where my father would have a place. And yet it had always been Grandfather who was thought of as the romantic, the exile for love, the man who had given up his country, while in a way the greatest sacrifice had been hers, because nobody had recognized it as such. She was as cut off from the Battacharis as Grandfather from the Fletchers. The remoteness of their respective families had nothing to do with distances.

'All the years I can remember, Grandfather and Father have told of England, and Portsmouth and Admiral Nelson, and Mr Churchill, and the Fletcher family. Never have I heard one story of Battacharis, only always of Fletchers.'

'Do not blame your father. England is far away and such places have magic, we do not see the reality. He only wanted to be like the ancestors of that place.'

'But he is not like, is he? And I am not like also. Our skin does not whiten because my father does not talk of the Battacharis.'

Grandmother did not respond. Eventually I said to her, 'Did you hear through the wall? I said things to him that he does not wish mentioned. Our colour, our race, our neighbours who pretend also that they do not belong in this country?'

Still Grandmother did not respond.

'My father is very angry that I have refused Gordon.'

'Child, he is hurt that is all. He cannot understand why you do not leap for the opportunity to go to the land of the Nelsons, Churchills and Fletchers.'

Sixth June, nineteen hundred and forty-four. We sat and talked quietly for a long time. Then I asked Grandmother to allow me to put on one of her saris. Later, draped and pleated in silk, I looked at my reflection. I said, 'This is the other half of me, the portion that I haven't known.' Grandmother removed the fire-opal earrings from her own ears and hooked them into mine.

In the memorial garden, the wind has dropped and the afternoon sun is warm on Anna's face. She sees Shalina at the pedestrian crossing waiting for the lights to change, then watches as she comes with the striding walk of a girl more used to wearing jeans than the sari.

'Phew!' She fans her face. 'I shan't be sorry to get this off. I know they're supposed to be floaty and cool and that . . . I expect it's me.' She laughs. 'We Pompey Zulfikars aren't used to this ethnic clobber.'

Anna laughs. Ah, what a grandchild to have.

'Anyway,' Shalina says, 'I don't want to spoil it, I want to keep it so that when you've gone back to India I shall have something to remind me of you and Mum's family.' She laughs again. 'To hear her talk you'd think there wasn't another family in the world like the Zulfikars.'

As Anna nods, the girasol, the exotic fire-opal, and silver earrings flash. She takes the jewels from her ears. Shalina is tall, she stoops as her grandmother hooks them into the pink earlobes.

'These will be better for remembering. Battachari, Fletcher, Zulfikar and soon perhaps Harrison?'

Shalina pretends a coy look, and shakes her head from side to side, feeling the long jewels flicking her cheeks.

The sun that shines across Portsmouth Harbour glitters the mica particles of the D-Day memorial and sets the girasol stones afire.

THE COFFEE BABY

THE COFFEE BABY

'That's it, dear. Up on the bed. Just want to have a look at your blood-pressure. Have a little see how you're coming along.'

For the sixth time that afternoon Sister Hanna Collins, fifty-nine, twelve stone and hard on her feet, flexed her fingers inside the surgical gloves before sliding them into the unyielding girl.

'Come on, love – relax. Just like at the clinic. Have a good deep breath. Out sl-ow-ly. That's the ticket. Just want to feel its little head.'

Han cocked her head, listening with her fingers.

'Oh yes, very nice. Not much happening at the moment, though. We'll have another little try later.'

The girl eased herself awkwardly from the hard mattress and gave a forced smile.

'All right then, love? You'll be all right. No problem. It'll be a piece of cake, you'll see.'

As Han removed the gloves they made a loud snap, and the girl gave a start.

'Goodness! Not nervous are you? Can't have my mothers being nervous.'

Han patted the girl with professional kindliness. She had uttered these phrases a thousand times to a thousand mothers. Rhetorical questions. 'Not nervous are you?', a denial that there was anything to be nervous about. Birth! It's only birth! Same way we all come into the world! A few challenges to her almost forty years of midwifery skill. But for all the groaning and thrashing about, all the head tossing, the calling for mothers and cursing of lovers, for the majority of Han's mothers, it was routine – a piece of cake. Within twenty-four hours they were sitting up pretty and perky and full of themselves with the experience of the labour-ward packed away in the subconscious.

The girl fingered the buttons of her pretty, print dressing-gown.

'It really doesn't hurt, does it.'

It wasn't a question and Han paused in her disposal of a paper sheet to look into the girl's face. She was just a kid. Eighteen? Nineteen. Not much more than a schoolgirl when you came to look at her. Long, brown hair, well-cut and shiny; smooth, fine skin and square, good teeth. She had always been fed the right foods this one. Strong as an ox! She was hunching her shoulders and clutched her right elbow with her left hand.

'I mean, really . . . not going to hurt. They said at the clinic . . .'

It was kind of pathetic really, the way she stood there, like a kid at school asking if a polio test hurt, not believing what she had been told at home.

'Well, not really. Depends on what you mean by hurt. You ever had a bad accident? Break a bone?'

The girl pushed back her sleeve and held out a scarred forearm.

'I went through a glass door when I was little.'

'Oh, nasty. Well, it's nothing like that. Makes your back ache. They never seem to tell you that at the clinic. Bad backache and hard work.'

Han held the girl's hand for an unprofessionally long moment.

'It's why it's called "labour" you know.'

Han relaxed her hold on the girl's hand, and the girl resumed her elbow-holding pose. Han glanced down at her watch. It had dangled from her uniform ever since her Dad had given it to her thirty-eight years ago.

'How's that for timing? Quarter past three. Just in time for the tea-trolley. Now you just slip off back down the ward and I'll look in on you later.'

In the small staff-room, furnished with the kind of furniture that is requisitioned rather than bought, where staff on duty could go for a cup of tea and a quick cigarette, Han sat for a while and chatted to the others about the retirement party they were arranging for her. It was odd how little she was affected, after nearly forty years on the wards she had expected to feel . . . well, she didn't know what, but something more than 'Ah well, only one more day to go'.

Back on the labour-wards the six beds were still in the possession of the same six women as earlier. First one, in for her sixth, thirty-eight, had the curtains drawn round her bed. Han poked her head round. Nothing happening. One other bed was occupied, the monitor blipping and the sound of the baby's heart both irritating and reassuring.

Women wandered about holding their arms like pegs, dragging and scuffing their feet. It was funny really, how one day they were out shopping, cooking, hoovering, then, as soon as they came in they walked about as though their bodies would shatter.

She reached the end of the ward and saw the young girl standing alone in the partitioned-off area where there was a television and a few armchairs.

'Anything happening?'

The girl shook her head.

'Ah well, that's how it goes. Often happens like that. Get a few niggly pains, you think it's all happening, soon as you see the hospital it all goes quiet again. Happens all the time.'

The girl was at the window looking down. Han went and stood by her. This was the old wing. It had survived the face-lift and massive extensions of some of the other buildings. Han had first looked down from this window, oh what . . . twenty years ago. The day after tomorrow she would probably never look down from it again. People always said they'd come back, pop in on the wards, but they never did. Nurses and patients alike, they never did.

Suddenly her reverie was disturbed by a small sound from the girl.

'Started up again?' Han asked.

The girl turned, flung herself upon Han and burst into tears. Han was used to tears – trickles, floods, streams, tears of joy, tears of depression. The girl sobbed once or twice as Han held her.

'Now, then, this won't do. You don't want to be all red-eyed at visiting time.' She offered a paper tissue and the girl wiped her face.

'Nobody's coming.'

'Well, never mind. You can come and sit with me if you like. Anyway, who knows, you might be busy by then.'

Han felt sorry for the little thing. It often happened in this town. Half the fathers were sailors. Off to sea when they were most needed. Why couldn't somebody in some department somewhere understand that it was more important for a man to be in at his child's birth than off firing some dummy rockets or guns or whatever it was sailors did these days?

'Your man in the navy?'

A few years ago Han would have asked 'Your husband in the navy?' but times had changed and there were a good number of her mothers now who came in without a wedding ring. Back when Han did her training, you never saw a woman without some sort of a ring on her marriage finger. On the whole, Han thought, these times were better. No more of that dreadful pretence about a husband who didn't really exist. Much better.

The girl ran a forefinger along her bottom lid and looked at the tear she collected.

'No, he's a student – we both are. He got knocked down last Saturday. He's in hospital, the other one.'

'Dear, oh dear. Not badly hurt?'

'Some bones broken, but not too bad.'

'That's good then. He'll be up and about in no time at all. Don't keep broken bones in bed long these days.'

'He was looking forward to it so much. We both were. He's been to all the classes with me. He does breathing exercises with me, read all the books . . . he said he would like to help deliver the baby . . . to be the first one to touch it . . . to start it off breathing. I would have liked that too but it isn't allowed, is it? But he was going to be in the delivery room . . . we had arranged that.'

'Well love, don't cry, don't upset yourself. Anyway, when you do start labour properly, it's just as likely you might be glad he's not there. It quite often happens, you'd be surprised. Lots of my mothers like to get on with it without any men about. Some of the dads chicken out at the last minute.'

'Jim wouldn't – he was so thrilled about the baby. He said it would probably be the most beautiful moment in our lives.'

'Anybody else coming to visit?'

'No. Well, maybe afterwards some of our friends from

the university. But nobody of mine, or Jim's. They all live abroad.' She hesitated. 'Actually they don't know about the baby yet. We decided we would take the baby to them and then they would see it and . . .' She pleated a piece of dressing-gown again and again, running it between her thumb and forefinger nails. 'When they see the baby they will just love it.'

A buzzer sounded. Han patted the girl and turned to go.

'Hundred to one that's our twins on their way. Now you go and wash your face and do some breathing exercises and I'll be along later.'

When Han came back on the ward, curtains were drawn round the girl's bed and a nurse was with her.

'It's all happening,' said the nurse. 'Mrs Patterson here is giving us some surprise, Sister. I'm just taking her in. She's coming along nicely.'

The girl's face was eager and alive. Quite different from the sad little face earlier.

'Sister . . . could you be there?'

'Oh, I'll be there all right, don't you worry.'

The nurse had gone on into the harshly-lit delivery-room. The girl said quietly, 'I know you're busy and all that, but could you be the one to deliver me? Be the first one to touch the baby?'

What was it about this bit of a girl? Han wagged her head indulgently.

'All right, then. Come on.'

'I've got a . . .' she went to her locker, 'tape-recorder. Would it be allowed if I took it in? It won't be the same, but at least Jim . . . if I kept it switched on when the baby comes.'

'You'll get me shot. Go on, bring it.'

Han went through the preparation routine, then sat down and took up the tape-recorder. Contractions punctuated their conversation.

'How much tape is there on?'

'It's a one-twenty. I thought two hours would be enough.'

'Hm, not a video, though, is it? Two hours of grunting and puffing won't tell your Jim much – except that you know a few more Anglo-Saxon words than he expected. Will you mind that?'

'He'd have heard them if he was here. I want it to be as near to him being here as I can.'

'I know what, how about me doing a commentary? Yes, that'd be really something for him to hear.' Han's face was alive with enthusiasm. 'I've always said I'd write a book when I retired. Never thought about this kind of thing. Hey, I could make features, radio, TV. Now, if we hang the mike here on the drip-hook . . . and . . . let me see, the recorder here . . . can you reach the switch?'

As the evening wore on, Han became totally absorbed in the coming baby, more than she had been with any delivery for years. There used to be times when she thrilled at the sight of a baby's head appearing, but that sight had become 'a head presenting' or sometimes 'anterior presentation' (which was interesting), occasionally a foot 'presented', when Han's skill and expertise were admired by anybody who worked with her.

Han was always pleased for her mothers when it was over. 'There you are,' she would say, 'that's what it was all about.' She liked the calm and restfulness for the few minutes when she and the mother drank sweet tea together, but for most of the time it had become routine – her job, one that she was good at, but still just her job. Yet, here, on almost the last shift of her career, with this little bit of a girl, Han had become animated and excited. If she could put some of that on record . . . well, it would be really good.

'Sister.' It was very near now but the girl lay restfully for a few moments. Han's hand went automatically to the switch. 'No, don't record this bit, but well . . . I just wanted you to know . . . because . . . you're West Indian aren't you?'

'Jamaican. I was. Long time ago now.'

'That's why I wanted you to be . . . Jim's from Grenada. That's why he wanted to be here. He called the baby the Coffee Baby. He said Coffee Babies need a real welcome into the world . . . to make up for some of the things later on.' She halted, closed her eyes and concentrated on her breathing.

'I wanted you to know.'

'Thank you,' said Han and squeezed the girl's hand not knowing what she could say that would sound adequate. This little family, one she had met for the first time a few hours ago, one in another hospital three miles away and the third – the secret still beneath her hand – touched a part of her she had forgotten existed.

She felt a great movement under her hand and saw the contraction rise on the monitor.

'Here we go.'

She reached over and switched the recorder on, and with more eloquence than anyone who knew Han could have believed her capable of, she spoke to the boy with the broken bones. She looked at the crown of the head as he would have done, saw the face emerge, saw the perfect hands and feet showing the only sign as yet of the boy's race, the purple-tinged nails, and heard the first round vowel of its cry.

SEEING THE VALLEY

SEEING THE VALLEY

As they reached the brow of the hill, the boy stretched his arm behind him and the girl clasped his outstretched fingers. The hill was not steep and she was used to climbing, so the gesture was an expression of his masculinity and a chance to touch again, if only chastely.

He waved his free hand theatrically, sweeping it across the skyline and down towards the valley.

'Well, there's my valley.'

The girl's eyes followed where he indicated.

Sixteen symmetrical avenues.

In every avenue twenty-four houses. Back-to-back, side-to-side.

Three hundred and eighty-four slate roofs, blackened by forty years in a wind, dust-laden from the pit-tip.

Three hundred and eighty-four chimneys, expelling trails of smoke into the July sunshine.

The avenues were built on a slope, giving the village the appearance of collapsed rows of dominoes. A squat church tower, sticking its finger into people's lives, intruded upon the regularity of the plan.

The sun, an interrogator's lamp, glared upon the village. Examined spoil heaps. Cross-examined ashy ringworm scars of the fierce combustion within, and illuminated the work-worn fabric of it all.

An alien place.

In her native county there were streams running clean from chalk hills, mellow houses, smoke in wisps, suitable church spires, and sheep, unobtrusive, on the downs.

His valley, his village, was inelegant and coarse. There was nothing to like, nothing to love.

A cloud lugged its shadow over the valley. The village softened.

Greys and browns of the slate and bricks became muted, and blended with the ling-covered hills and the spoil from the pits. In the more sombre light it had character, was alive. A place of work where people didn't go in for affectation, status and rank, or the order of peck that ruled her village.

The boy was watching her closely. She knew that he would be. His eyes moved quickly, searching every part of her face. She wanted to say something that would please him, but did not know what.

'Real Lawrence country, isn't it?'

The boy lifted her fingers to his lips, moving his head from side to side. She could not decide whether he was shaking his head in disagreement or enjoying the contact of lips and fingers.

'This could be the . . .' she faltered, confused by his smile, 'you know, the place that Lawrence wrote about. The story about the place with a secret white hawthorn bush, and he took her there to make love to her, and couldn't make it.'

The fascination of opposites. She by his directness, he by her reserve. When light-heartedly mocking he emphasized his broad accent.

'D'st like the village, then?'

She smiled, slightly. 'It's . . . quite romantic.'

He turned her face towards him holding her chin. 'There's none like you there.' He clasped an arm about her shoulder. 'See there?' He pointed to the nearest pit-tip where tubs spewed shale on to the irregular top of the heap.

'If it hadn't been for my dad, that tip would have been a pound or two heavier. He brought a bit home with him every day, him in his lungs. And see there?' He pointed to a heap streaked and green-tinged with age.

'Somewhere in there is Old Man Merrit. Used to live next me grandma. He was picking coal in the General Strike – the crust collapsed. Cremated free and for nothing. It's burnt out long since. And just under here's the Salla Kenna seam. Ton after ton of best coal, and twenty-four men nobody could get out when it flooded. I was fourteen. I told my mam I'd not go down – ever. And she said not to worry she wasn't going to let me. She said I should try for the grammar school. D'you know I was the first lad from the village ever went into the pit offices. Nobody liked it much.'

He laughed. 'When I started there my dad took me on one side, said he wanted to talk to me. I thought he was going to say to me, now I was a man with a pay packet, to be careful not to catch anything from Catty-Ann who lived on bottom road, handy for men coming up from work. But what he said to me was, if I ever let on to Mam what he earned, he'd belt the daylights out of me.'

Her eyes did not leave his face while he spoke. Her cheeks were flushed, she felt awkward, embarrassed.

'I'm sorry,' she said.

He laughed and brushed her ear with his lips. 'Why sorry?'

'So stupid going on about Lawrence . . . and being romantic . . .'

He interrupted. 'But it is! It is! Down there are people baking apple pies, learning to read, making love, some dying, some idiots frittering away their lives, some people, like my mam, saying "get out of it" to their kids. They aren't any better or worse or less romantic than the ones Lawrence wrote about.'

He took her by the waist and pulled her running down the hill.

At the bottom they stopped, breathless and laughing. The boy lifted a strand of hair from her forehead.

'Bie, but th's pretty.'

Tugging at her arm he led her along the dusty track through gorse and rough moorland.

'Come on, I'll show you something.'

'Another pit-tip?'

'I'll show you better than that. I'll show you Lawrence's secret bush. It wasn't a hawthorn. It was white, wild roses. I know my Lawrence. He wasn't the only one whose mam sent him to the grammar school.'

She wished she was more like him. Wished to be as assured and confident. He didn't really need her approval of his village. He would have liked it if she had done so, but it was not important, it was not a condition of his approval of her.

'And I'll tell you something else about old Lawrence. If he'd have had you with him when he found the roses, his story would have had a different ending.'

THE GOLD-WIDOW

THE GOLD-WIDOW

Mabotho Majoro was later than she intended. She had planned to rise before dawn, but already the sky showed faint pink through the hut window.

She unwound herself from the sleeping-blanket quietly, so as not to rouse the children, and then placed it neatly rolled against the wall. She dipped a mug into the drinking-water can, drank to freshen herself and fill her stomach, then stepped outside to fetch sticks.

Standing for a moment in the sharp dawn air, Mabotho Majoro looked critically at the hut. There was not much of the thatch left; as it disintegrated she had done what she could with bits of corrugated-iron. The corn-coloured mud walls showed old cracks, patches and a lot of new crazing. The children were for ever idly picking and picking at the loose surface. She would have liked to have repaired both roof and walls before Samu came home from the city, but there was always too much other work, in the fields and on her own mealie plot and vegetable garden.

A handful of dry twigs and grass soon brought the fire to life. Mabotho filled a black pot with water and set it above the flames. From the mealie-sack she took the last of the white kernels, threw them into the pot and stirred with her hand until the water took on a milky look.

She padded back and forth cleaning the hut and yard but could not give it her full attention. The water she had drunk on rising had been only a short-term pacifier, and now the smell of the softening mealies made her hungry, so she shook some tea from a packet into a tin mug and poured on to it some of the bubbling mealie-water. Normally she would have boiled the tea for ten minutes to get the full strength from the leaves, but today she waited only long enough for the leaves to sink.

She took the drink to the door and sat down on the rough stone step. Thin trails of smoke rose from under other black iron pots as other women started preparing mealie-pap or porridge or boiled mealie-meal. The sky was glowing now, soon the sun would rise to bake the vegetable plots even harder. But today Mabotho Majoro would not be jarring her joints as she hoed between rows of corn.

The slapping walk of a woman not wearing shoes came near. Malokisang. Returning home after working all night in the shebeens and beer-halls she owned. Malokisang came and sat on the step and punched Mabotho playfully on the thigh.

'So! Republic Day is here again. The day when Samu has said he will honour his village wife with a visit.'

Mabotho smiled at her childhood friend.

'Republic Day is the day when Samu comes.'

'Oh yes – Samu always comes.' Malokisang rolled her eyes skywards. 'Did he come last Republic Day?'

'The tsotsis stole all his money. He would have come.'

'Well bless the tsotsis. At least you have no child at the breast this Republic Day.'

Malokisang had always been the same, forthright, going right to the heart of any subject. Touching nerves.

'This day he will come.' Mabotho handed tea to

Malokisang who took a long drink and with a screwed-up mouth held out the mug.

Mabotho shook her head.

'Ach. I have told you a thousand times, when you are in need of sugar, ask Malokisang. Did we not go through initiation together? Did you not hold me when I would have run and shamed my mother? Did I not comfort you after the cutting? I will give you sugar!'

'Tomorrow we shall have sugar.'

'Tomorrow, tomorrow you will have many thing.' Malokisang's gold front tooth glinted in the rising sun as she elbowed Mabotho, laughing quietly so as not to waken the children.

Malokisang had a coarse humour, but it was a small fault. There was very much goodness, much warm-heartedness in her. She had not been like this before she went to work in the city. She had never talked about it, but Mabotho knew that she had experienced imprisonment for not carrying her Passbook and abusing a police officer. These days Malokisang was fat and jolly, though her eyes were no longer soft, and she was prosperous now – a Shebeen Queen – the owner of beer-halls.

She looked Mabotho up and down. Abruptly she said, 'You are very thin.'

'You say this all the time.'

'I think Samu does not send you money?'

'He sends money.'

It was almost true. Samu did send her money, but the intervals had become so long that it was now many months since the last instalment came.

'Muh! I tell you my girl, I know you are thin. I say that you have become a gold-widow – I say your man Samu has taken a city wife, and will not come home.'

'Samu will come. If he has a city wife, still he will come.'

'Did he come last year when it was Republic Day? Did he? Don't look away like that – I know he never came! Those men who go to the gold mines, take to the city life. If they have a wife there and children, they cannot afford village families as well.'

'Samu earns very much money in the gold mines,' Mabotho said quietly.

'Ha! – and Samu has also learned how to spend much money! I saw him when he came last time (three years ago – you see? I know when he came!). Ho, what a sight! Shiny pants – tight – with zip! A coat with red lines (I tell you that coat cost plenty!) and a blue hat with many cords around it.'

Mabotho did not need her friend to tell her how Samu had been dressed. She could have described every square inch of cloth, every pearly shirt-button and every tiny hole that made patterns on the toes of his shoes. Samu had looked beautiful – finer than any other man returning from the city.

Malokisang wagged her head like a grandmother.

'Cords on his hat! Ha! How is that going to fill the bellies of his family here? I tell you, they are all the same, these men.'

Suddenly her voice became gentle again. 'Why do you not come, as I have asked many times? Come and help me at the shebeens. I could do with a girl like you. I could trust you. It is not the life one would choose, but then who lives such a life? And it is better than pushing a hoe all day. Look! I see your chest bones – do you see bones like that on me?'

She thrust forward her bosom, stretching the bright pink dress and straining the gilt buttons and patted her healthy black skin.

'If you come, I would pay you good money. It would

make me happy, because we are friends and you would get more fatness, be more woman.'

Mabotho felt shamed by her grey, dull skin when compared with Malokisang's rich body in its pink dress, and the plump legs in their red stockings.

'Samu will come this time.'

'So – Samu will come this time. And if he comes this time – will he come next time? Will the time between the money-sending get longer and longer until there is no money?'

Mabotho hung her head. Did everybody know that Samu had stopped sending money home? That she worked from dawn till sundown, hoeing her own maize plot then working for a few cents on the plots of others – and still scarcely enough money to feed the children?

Malokisang put a plump arm round Mabotho's thin shoulder.

'Don't hang your head like that! You should be proud. You are fine, you are the provider for the children. Look around this village. What do you see? It is the women who keep the children from hunger. The men go to the city – all right, they must go, there is no living to be made here, I know this – but how many return? The young boys without wives come once – and never again. Here they cannot get hats with cords! And the ones with village wives? Ah yes, they mean to come. Sometimes they do come – they bring pretty things from the city and leave behind them yet another mouth to feed.'

Mabotho could not argue. It was true, she could have wept for the truth of it. But not Samu. Malokisang did not know Samu so well. Samu would come.

Behind the two women, inside the hut, came sounds of the children awakening. Little Tenta tottered to the doorway, blinking at the light. Malokisang picked him up and kissed his bare belly. 'Ah, here is the result of the last Republic Day visit.' The little boy squirmed with pleasure at the tickling, the feel of the silky dress and plump body.

'Ach. To think that there will be a day when some girl will believe that her life is incomplete without this little thing here. And all it is fit for is making mouths to feed.' She petted and kissed him, making him giggle with delight, then put him down and took the girls one on each side and enclosed them in the circles of her arms and sang them a slightly bawdy song in a deep voice.

At last Malokisang stretched herself. 'Ah, Mabotho,' she said, 'it's time we forgot the men. Let them go to shine the shoes of white men and dig his gold. We are as strong as they are. Do you not work hard, all day, every day? Where is your hat with many cords? I tell you my girl, you should come and work for me. I will give you regular work, easy work. You will wear pretty dresses like this. You can buy education for the children. Think how it would be – they could become teachers, or nurses, or doctors! Especially the girls. What will it be for them in twenty years? Also waiting for husbands in coats with red lines, who come and fill their bellies with children, when they need them filled with food?'

Mabotho had heard Malokisang's argument before today.

'Samu will buy education for the children,' she said. 'When he comes back, all will be well again, you see.' She smiled shyly. 'When Samu came last here, he said that he will bring me shoes with high heels and open at the toes, and red varnish for my toenails. He has promised me.'

'My! To remind him of city women no doubt!' Malokisang hauled herself to her feet. 'Well, when the train comes and Samu does not, I will be waiting – and you will join the Tribe of the Women. You see.' And she padded off giving Mabotho a playful smack. 'These men are good for just one thing. Buying my beer!'

Mabotho went back to the hut, and in less than an hour she and the children were on their long walk to town, to wait for the train that would bring Samu.

By the time they reached the station the sun was high and Mabotho had to carry Tenta on her back for the last mile or so. The usual waiting place for blacks was a patch of rough ground close by the railway track, and it was there that the family settled to await the arrival of the train.

Soon the children were hungry, and Mabotho divided a small flat loaf between them. But as they ate, their eyes were fixed upon the sweet-smelling cobs sizzling on the charcoal fire of the mealie-seller. Suddenly Mabotho unknotted the end of her scarf and took out a few cents.

'Here, let us have some fun today. Buy mealies – and see that they are fat and well-roasted!'

Tozama, being the eldest, took the money and Mabotho watched as she and 'Mimi' discussed the mealies like women in the market, ignoring Tenta who watched the deal wide-eyed.

They shared the hot cobs and, watching their enjoyment, Mabotho relaxed. Later on she handed out a few more of her precious cents and they all had tins of icy Coke and oranges. She was playful and they played silly games, arousing in Tozama hazy memories of times before 'Mimi' and Tenta, before Mother had to go every day to the maize fields and she, Tozama, had become the little mother to the other two.

As the day wore on, more people arrived. The white ones sat in the shade of the waiting-room, the black ones on the rough ground.

A number of women, wearing bright, Western-style

hats, shoes and coloured stockings, came and lounged beneath some trees. They smoked cigarettes and chattered among themselves. A few boys idled about them, showing off, flicking cigarette-ends in an arc to show how street-wise they were. The women were too expensive for them, but at least they could look.

Mabotho recognized several women who used to live in a nearby village before they set themselves up in town. Some were of her own age and a few older.

Like her they too had children, had once waited for husbands to come back from the mines.

Like her they had once been skinny and scrappily dressed. She did not make any judgements. When things got hard, apart from a vegetable plot and a few sticks of furniture, few women had more than the use of their own flesh to sell. Mabotho thought they must be very strong to do that. She could never do that. Take any drunk, half-wit or bully with a rand or two in his pocket. But village wives who became gold-widows must do what they can.

Mabotho seldom had the time or energy to think of anything except whatever chore she was working at. But now, placidly waiting for Samu to arrive, she let her mind wonder about the future.

She watched Tozama chewing the pith off an orange skin. What if Samu did not buy an education for the girls, would they finish up hoeing fields, or going away to be servant-girls in the cities, perhaps leaving their children for Mabotho to bring up? Those women in the hats, some old grandmother was probably seeing to the children.

A chilling vision came. Her own future, an endless grind of mouths to feed, months waiting for money from the city, years waiting for trains.

This time she would be strong with Samu. He must see how important the children's education was. It occurred to her that if the girls became nurses they need never take a husband.

She began to think of things in a new way. No husbands. No lobolo. Not to be sold by the father to the husband. She had never before thought of a dowry in that light. What difference was there between the money paid by the drunks and half-wits, and lobolo paid by a husband? A woman was bought from the father by the husband. A woman was bought! When a man married he bought a home, an animal or two and a wife. And the wife ended up with three children and a hoe. At least the women under the trees kept their money. Or did they? Mabotho wasn't sure. Quite possibly there was some man, somewhere, getting something out of it, it seemed to be the way of things. She hoped that the women kept the money. They deserved it, doing that!

Revolutionary thoughts for Mabotho. Malokisang was often telling how gold-widows should make better lives for themselves and their children, but it was always after the men had left them. A nurse need never have to take a husband! A nurse could own herself!

Down the line the approaching train hooted. At once there was bustling and chatter. People began to move towards the railway-track.

The train pulled to a halt and passengers began to alight. Standing apart, with Tozama, 'Mimi' and Tenta at her skirts, Mabotho searched among the black passengers for Samu. She saw a few men who she knew worked with Samu. She made a move towards one who had brought her a message last year, telling how the tsotsis had stolen Samu's money and he could not get back to the village this year. Why did he suddenly turn away? She was certain that he had seen her. Soon there was nobody left on the rough ground except herself and the women under the trees bargaining with men in city suits.

Samu had not come.

Mabotho suddenly held out her hands to the girls. 'Come! This is the first day of education. First! I tell you remember this day. This hot day when we walked from the village and waited for the train from the city, and nobody came. Next!' She looked at their serious little faces, holding back on the laughter that wanted to come bubbling out. Then 'Mimi' jigged with excitement and Tenta copied her, not knowing why except that there was something nice going on. Tozama was old enough not to get excited until she knew there was something to get excited about. 'Next, we shall have Coke and . . . hot-dogs. Then! We shall go back to the village. And I shall learn to sell beer and you shall learn to write and do numbers.'

Soon the bulging dusty village bus halted in a cloud of dust, and Mabotho gave a handful of cents to the driver as though she had all the money in the world. On the bus she hugged her children.

An emotion she did not understand began to flow through her. She did not understand it because it was new to her. For the first time she felt the elation of freedom.

Well, freedom of a kind.

THE COMPANY WIFE

THE COMPANY WIFE

Liz raised her arms and stretched her legs, making an X of her body, and stared through the fancy leaves and flowers of the burglar-proofing at the alien constellations of the southern hemisphere. On other nights she had lain like this, trying to fix the pattern of stars in her mind, but they remained random.

Back home there were familiar patterns in the night sky.

'Dear Mum,
'In Africa mid-summer is in December and the night sky is just what I had imagined it would be. It reminds me of those dark pansies that Gran grows by her front door. The stars appear very bright, like bits of Christmas-tree decoration . . .'

Beside her in the rumpled bed, John breathed deep and gentle. He worked long hours on the high, dusty sun-stricken veldt, he came to bed early and slept soundly. Not Liz, though, she had little to do all day to tire her. Just the duties of an overseas company wife. Shopping, deciding on menus for entertaining visiting members of the board from the UK, taking their wives round the city. Everybody on expenses. Liz was on expenses. She had dreary coffee and dull tea with other company wives. The old ennui.

'. . . and if you are invited to someone's house for Sunday tea, you often find the servant wearing a white uniform with scarlet turban and sash. They carry round cucumber sandwiches and silver teapots. It must have been like this a hundred years ago back home – if you were well off . . .'

Liz smiled, imagining her mother's apparent casualness when she asked the aunts if they wanted to read Lizzie's latest letter. Liz never exaggerated in her letters, it was not necessary. The company provided. Chauffeur, uniformed nanny, flat in the suburbs, with services and a swimming pool. There had been a time when the aunts had looked down on Liz's mum, it still hurt. It did them no harm to have a little of Liz's temporary affluence pushed under their noses.

Flinging an arm across her face, John turned over and muttered in his sleep. Immediately on contact, sweat sprang where their skin touched. She pushed him further to his part of the bed and turned on her side to watch the stars. The crickets seemed louder now than in the early evening. The night was filled with their grating and sawing, the garden must be seething. She imagined row on row of them, like the soldier ants that were for ever invading the larder.

'. . . and you'd be surprised, Dad, how easy it is to let the sound of insects get on your nerves once you start to think about it.

I always become aware of crickets just after sundown. Perhaps that is when they start up or simply that I don't actually hear them until the boys have gone to bed. But at sundown I become conscious of them. Before I came here, I associated the sound of cicadas with balmy tropic evenings, a delightful background of natural sound. Wherever did I get that idea I wonder? I hate them. Isn't that ridiculous? How can one hate insects? Hate is . . .'

It was too hot for philosophical rumination about hate. Liz lifted the thin sheet with one foot and allowed it to drift down, trying to move air over her body. The air moved, but it was not cooling.

As Liz raised herself on one elbow so as to turn the pillow on to its cooler side, there came from the servants' rooms high on the roof of Dunkeld Court, the next-door block of flats, the sound of shuffling bare feet and a whispered argument. A door-latch rattled. Someone in high heels clicked hurriedly up stone steps. A bead curtain rattled. A door creaked shut, then all was quiet again.

Liz recognized the bead curtain. It hung at the door of the windowless cell that was home of Ezekiel, the Zingili boss-boy of Dunkeld Court. Whenever Zeke went in or out of his room and Liz was on her balcony, he would shout 'Heya!' grinning his perfect white teeth at her. A white man would have given a low whistle. Any possible misinterpretation of his gesture was negated by the respectful sweep of his tattered sugar-planter hat, 'Good morning, M'em.'

As she did frequently on hot nights, Liz got out of bed. Carefully. John didn't know that there were many hours when he slept alone. Sometimes she would go into the sitting room and read until it was nearly dawn. She went quietly with bare feet, recognizing her own childishness in ignoring Sara's wagging finger, 'The Medam must not wear the bare feet, even in the flet. The jiggers will eat the toes.'

As she went to switch on a lamp, Liz remembered that there was nothing to read, the library books were stacked ready to go back in the morning, she had read both newspapers from cover to cover, and Sara had taken all the magazines with her back home to Soweto. She wandered about, the rooms lit by the reflected light of bright security lamps in the corridors, idly plumping up cushions and gathering up an odd toy or two. She looked in at the children, wishing she could always feel like this about them, that she could be better at coping, calmer in their quarrels.

She wandered into the kitchen.

Liz quite liked this kitchen. Although the company had installed the gleaming and expensive equipment, Liz had managed to make it a bit like her kitchen back home, with plants and baskets of fruit and some wooden furniture. She rarely had the place to herself except, as now, in the middle of the night. There were sometimes as many as four Africans as well as herself, all doing the work she did unaided in her own house back home. But the Africans, like John, were paid by the company. Liz liked their uncomplicated friendliness and willingness and was grateful that they accepted her in the kitchen which was, after all, their territory.

Taking a pot of yoghurt from the refrigerator, she hoisted herself on to the work surface beside the wide window. It was thirty feet above street level and, as it had no balcony or foothold, it was the only window in the flat uncluttered by iron-leafed burglar-proofing. Below ran the broad road to Pretoria.

'Dear Mum,

'I wish I could show you the road where we live. You would love all the colour. It's an avenue divided down the centre by a wide strip of grass which is kept watered, clipped short and wonderfully neatly edged. There are beds of flaming canna lilies, and great clumps of nerines and millions of Livingstone daisies. The clumps of asparagus fern – like the one on your sideboard – grow in the open and are six feet across and almost as high. In each flowerbed is a palm tree. Best of all, though, is the tree that grows just opposite where I often sit (in the kitchen) and think about what I shall write to you. It is a jacaranda tree – enormous – as big as an oak tree and the same shape, the blossom comes when the branches are bare, clear lilac . . .'

Liz took the lid off the yoghurt and removed the thin pad of mould that covered the top.

'. . . I don't think I told you the story about the yoghurt did I, Mum? Well our doctor told me that I ought to give it to the children and eat plenty myself. The first day it was delivered, every pot I opened was covered with mould. I rang up the dairy manager and told him exactly what I thought about it. Was my face red! It's supposed to be like that. The stuff they sell back home is just junk. I now have a passion for the stuff . . .'

She smiled, wondering if she would get one of her mother's diplomatically phrased letters – not wanting to interfere, Liz was very capable of course, but maybe to be just that extra bit careful, the hot weather and all that. It was quite nice to be fussed over by your Mum – as long as you were the other side of the world.

The smooth cream. Acidic, sharp. Below the avenue. Something moved. At first she thought it might be one of the scraggy dogs that wandered about scavenging, but no, over by the jacaranda she could make out the shape of a man. He was white, she saw his face and hands in the shadow of the tree.

He looked up and Liz moved quickly back from the window. He was not looking in her direction, though, but towards Dunkeld Court. He stepped out from the shelter of the tree and beckoned, first up, then down the road. From behind some palm trees, two more men came into view. They ran, crouching like monkeys, to the jacaranda. All three withdrew into the shadow and stood immobile. Liz kept as still as they. The formica surface began to feel hot and sticky through her thin wrap. She kept well back from the window and took little tastes of yoghurt, and watched.

It was seldom that one saw the avenue so empty. The five little shops on the corner that had been alive with people right up until midnight, were now shuttered, the only sign of life came from the patisserie where they were getting croissants ready for the first customers just after dawn.

'. . . I do quite a lot of my shopping in the small shops. There is a greengrocer – it's interesting about greengrocer shops, they smell so different from ones back home. I think it is the guavas and paw-paws that give off a powerful smell – rather nauseating. Mostly Portuguese . . .'

A light momentarily caught the canna lilies, flaring them alight, then went off. A car came coasting down the incline of the road.

'. . . I'll tell you something quite interesting. Even on the very hottest nights, for a short while the air clears and it gets cool. I don't know about in the heart of the city, but it happens out here in the suburbs. The crickets . . .'

The crickets had stopped again and there was no movement anywhere. Suddenly the car engine roared into life and the car was driven away very fast out of the city. As it pulled away, Liz saw that the three white men were racing across the wide avenue. They jumped a low garden wall and crouched immediately below where Liz sat. One man gave silent directions to the other two, one of whom went into the underground carpark and the other in at the 'Residents Only' entrance to Dunkeld. The man giving directions then went into an alley-way.

Liz jumped down and ran silently through the flat into the sitting room. She pressed herself into the folds of the curtains and watched. From there she could see the other end of the alley-way and all five levels of corridors with immaculate front doors, where lamps only six feet or so apart were kept burning all night.

The man held the alley-way door slightly open, looking up and waiting. Against the darkness of the sky appeared the darker shape of a second man, he must be the one who had gone in at the front door of Dunkeld and up on to the roof where there were washing-lines. He signalled a thumb-up. The alley-way man replied. For a short while neither moved.

The ground at the back of the flats was much higher than at the front where the kitchen was, so that where Liz now stood she was almost level with the two men. She jumped when the man who had gone into the carpark appeared only a foot or two below where she stood. He ran across a flowerbed, leapt a hedge and joined the man in the alley-way.

The crickets were silent.

Very faintly Zeke's bead curtain rattled, then Zeke came to the edge of his balcony, his pale servant's uniform showing up clearly. He could have reached up and touched the shoes of the man on the roof. But he did not look up. It was just like being at the pictures when you were a child – Liz wanted to warn Zeke, 'Look out! He's behind you!'

'Do you remember me telling you about Zeke who is so nice to the children. He gave them some goldfish and some wind-chimes . . .'

Zeke made a beckoning motion at the bead curtain and a woman came out. Liz recognized her. Annie-moo the other women called her. She was large and beautiful and accentuated the size of her breasts and curve of her hips with glossy, gathered dresses. She was very black-skinned and kept her hair in dozens of thin, beaded plaits. In cold weather she wore a coat made from the skin of dik-dik or some such animal. Liz had always assumed she was a prostitute from the way the men whooped at her and the women lowered their eyelids and jerked their chins as they turned from her. Liz wasn't very good at recognizing many of the tribal features but Annie-moo had a good voice.

'Have you ever heard of the Xhausa tribe? They are fascinating to listen to. Their language contains a lot of "clocking" sounds, made at the back of the palate. I've tried to do it but all I manage to do is send all the African women I try it on into fits of giggles. And if you've ever seen six or seven African women laughing at a white Madam who they think is a bit eccentric . . .'

Annie-moo and Zeke stood back against the wall, not

moving. The three white men did not move. Liz watched from behind her burglar-proofed window.

The crickets started again.

There was a sudden, quick flurry of movement and Zeke and the woman went hurrying down the steps. There was a cry followed by a clang. The man on the roof had fallen from the iron ladder down which he was clambering. Zeke and the woman began to run along one of the residents' corridors. The man in the alley-way came into the open and shouted, 'Hold it boy!' and took a stance with his hand-gun like an American TV cop. The third man ran up some steps and along the corridor towards Zeke and Annie-moo.

Zeke shouted something in what sounded like Zulu and the woman leapt from the balcony. Two shots zipped into the night. The woman shouted obscenities in English and Afrikaans from the flowerbed. The man who had come down from the roof prodded Zeke in the back until they were all together in the garden just below where Liz stood. Zeke and Annie-moo were handcuffed and pushed along the servants' alley.

Liz did not move for a long time.

If you believed everything you heard at dinners and cocktail parties, there were terrorists and subversives in every home and backyard. Liz had seen more handcuffs, revolvers and chases in the short time that she had lived here, than she would have believed possible.

She pressed her forehead hard into one of the iron leaf-shapes, suppressing tears and the fear.

Only twenty-eight more months and it will all be over.

Say that every day for the next thirty days then – Only twenty-seven more months and it will all be over.

She pushed down the images of Zeke and Annie-moo. She would think about them, but not yet, not tonight.

The air became hot again, but at least the crickets were silent. The pansy darkness began to show the first sign of dawn. She went back through the flat and into the bedroom, fingering the imprint of the iron leaf on her forehead.

John was still sleeping. Liz slid back under the sheet. The stars were less bright.

'Dear Mum,

'In the letter I got from you yesterday, you said that you often worry about us. You really mustn't you know. We are perfectly OK. This is a big, modern city, with police and buses and everything, just like home.'

The automatic tea-maker clicked on.

THE ZULU GIRL

THE ZULU GIRL

Eddie did not see the girl come or know how long she had been standing there. The colour of her dress blended with the bare red twigs of the thorn bushes as she stood, quite still, watching the only bit of civilization visible on the high veldt – the construction site where his gang was erecting a tall steel tower.

He was intrigued, not at the sight of a young woman in tribal dress near the site, it was common for women to come in search of their men; often they came in small groups, shrill voices sounding raucous to English ears, cluttered with bundles they would descend upon the site; the labourers would stop work and call out invitations like gangs of young men anywhere. What intrigued Eddie about this woman was the way she stood, still and silent, on a slight rise in the ground from which she had a view over the entire site.

She was tall and dignified in the manner of many Zulus, she had an air of remoteness and looked as though she could stand like that for days.

Eddie's African chargehand came over.

'What does she want, Altheus?' Eddie asked.

'Who knows?' Altheus drew up his shoulders into an exaggerated shrug, holding them high for several seconds before releasing them.

'How long has she been there?'

'Maybe a day, maybe more. Yesterday she was in the bush. Do not bother, Baas.'

'Do not bother, Baas' was as near as Altheus would go to telling the white man it was none of his business. Eddie nodded and went away to the other end of the site to supervise the erection of some steelwork and thought no more about the Zulu woman until he answered the call of the tea-boy banging on the corrugated shed.

He took his mug of tea and walked a little way towards the rise where the woman stood. A group of huge aloes gave a little shade from the noon sun, so Eddie pushed back into the cool leathery leaves and sat sideways-on to the woman who was standing in profile to him and he could see her more clearly now. Her skin was not light as he had first thought, but smeared with a kind of grey chalk, her natural darkness showing in streaks where sweat had run. She wore a long cotton-print skirt, voluminous and reaching almost to her ankles which were banded with coils of metal and beadwork. Looped about her shoulders was a large crimson cloak-like affair edged with intricate black tracery. On her head a high tubular hat of the same colour as the cloak.

She made a small sharp movement, bringing her hands up from her sides and clasping them beneath her belly. She was pregnant, near her time. Eddie guessed that she was no more than about eighteen. She must be aware that he was looking at her but she gave no indication. He ought to do something but could not think what, so he finished his tea and walked back to the steel-erectors.

The working day on the site began at dawn so as to get as much as possible of the heavy work done before the sun turned the dish-shaped site into an oven, so by two o'clock

Eddie had finished for the day and was in his Range Rover heading back into the city. As he left the site he turned towards the thorn bushes – she had gone. That evening he asked Molly, a Xhosa woman who helped in the house, if she could guess why the Zulu girl was standing by the thorn bushes out in the veldt.

'Perhaps she is widow, Masta,' Molly said. 'Some people make white face for widow, put fire-ashes on the face.'

'But why would she want to come to the site? If she is a widow then she wouldn't be looking for one of my men. Anyway, why just stand there?'

Molly gave the same slow shrug of the shoulders as Altheus had given earlier.

'Who knows?' she said. Her eyes and face were expressionless and like Altheus she implied, 'Do not bother, Baas – mind your own business.'

Next day Eddie was back on site just after sunrise. He had bumped the Range Rover over several miles of rough track beside the truck-load of men. As they reached the site the truck-driver roared ahead jolting the men about and they whooped and shouted like boys at a fun-fair. Suddenly they went very quiet and looked solemnly down as they passed the place where the silent girl now stood.

She had come down from the thorn thicket on the rise, and was now standing beside the track that led to the site. She stood in the same pose as before, her crimson cloak moving slightly in the morning air and her cotton skirt flapping gently against her body. Her belly was flat. Eddie expected to see the baby slung on her back, but it was neither there nor anywhere that he could see.

He stopped and got out.

'Are you looking for someone?'

Up to the moment that Eddie came to stand before her, she had not taken her eyes from the site but as he spoke she turned them slightly in his direction; her face as impassive as ever, and the stillness about her was almost tangible, chill. She looked into Eddie's eyes for about five seconds then returned her gaze to the site.

'Can you understand me?'

She didn't respond.

'Look, if you want something, say so. I don't like to see you there so long.'

Still there was no response.

Eddie stood for a moment or two longer then returned to the Range Rover where Altheus sat, his face rigid, like a fake ebony head in a tourist shop.

Neither man spoke until Eddie gave Altheus the work schedule for the day. Altheus took instruction politely but with few words, then he went off leaving Eddie feeling tense and fidgety. He went into the shack which served as his site office and sat looking out, she was exactly opposite. He knew that the reflection of light on the window made it impossible to see inside, so he sat on a stool gazing out at her.

Presently Altheus came into the shack with a stores requisition form to be signed. Eddie tried to make his remark casual as he applied his signature.

'That girl – she's still hanging about then.'

'Yes, I see this too.'

'Look, Altheus, it's none of my business if she stands where she is till the crack of doom, but if it's got any connection with the site or anybody on it – then it is my business.'

Altheus concentrated on folding the requisition form into a precise square, running each fold between thumb and fingernail, and said nothing.

'Is this a holy place or something? Does a spirit live here?'

'It is not that, Baas.'

'Not what?'

'Not a holy place.'

'Nothing to do with the site?'

'No, it is not that.'

Eddie could tell that if he was not careful he would become involved in one of those question and answer sessions that were always fruitless when Africans wanted to keep their own counsel, but Eddie was sure that the Zulu girl had something to do with his site, or somebody on it. Altheus knew it too. He left the office politely and correctly. Eddie continued to sit and gaze out of the window. The woman had moved now and gone back to her original position beside the thorn bushes. He sat on in the shack all day doing odd bits of paper-work and checking drawings, time and again looking out at the still, red figure on the rise.

Eddie was about to pack up for the day when he saw the woman suddenly leave her post and walk purposefully down to where a group of Africans were assembling a piece of equipment; they were huddled together, not aware that she was approaching. When she was within some yards of them she threw back her cloak in a dramatic gesture. He half expected to hear her shout, or wail, or cry. Her movements registered in detail. Frame by frame. She had a gun in her hand. A gun. He watched. She raised the weapon. Bracelets moved. Her arm jerked. Her body began to go off balance. She checked herself, he saw her anklebone whited as she brought herself upright once more. A man made a movement. Head back and arms reaching out he fell. Slowly, slowly.

Then Eddie flung open the shack door and raced across the yard. The Africans, too, had been momentarily stunned into inaction and silence, then as Eddie reached them they began shouting and flailing their arms at one another. Other men left their work and ran to see what had happened.

By the time Eddie reached the scene there were about twenty men staring down at the dead man. The girl was again still and impassive. A few notes of a song repeated themselves, '. . . drew a gun and . . .' He felt embarrassed at the association of ideas, but had a strong desire to whistle the line aloud, '. . . drew a gun and shot . . .' Suddenly some men started towards her aggressively.

'Leave her!' Eddie shouted with all the authority of a white boss and the men automatically obeyed, then stood together in small groups watching.

Eddie went to the girl and, clutching her arm, led her to the office shack. She went, her back straight, her chin raised. He took her inside.

'Stop there!' He pointed to the stool.

She had no intention of moving, any more than she had done for the past few days, but not knowing what the men might do, he locked her in and went back to the men.

The dead man lay on his side, his mouth half open, his eyes wide. A quick way to go. One moment tightening steel bolts, the next floored. Where the bullet had entered his chest was a neat disc, a third nipple. His back was a mess. There was a wide pool of blood in the yellow dust and already insects had been drawn to it.

'Get something to cover him.'

'What, Baas? What to cover him?'

'Anything. Just get him covered up.' Nobody moved.

'Move! One of you fetch a blanket, sack or something, from my car.' Still nobody moved.

'Well, what are you waiting for?'

One of the older men asked, 'Who shall go, Baas?'

'Does it . . .? Never mind.' He went himself and

fetched a rough blanket and threw it over the dead man.

'Better get the police now.'

'Yes, Baas.'

'Otherwise we shall be here all night.'

'Yes, Baas.'

Eddie glanced in the direction of the shack but the reflected sky was a cataract on the eye of the window, '. . . and from under her velvet gown . . .' Momentarily the men followed his gaze then turned back to the feet in thick-soled sandals that protruded from the blanket.

'Well? Hasn't anybody got anything to say before I go and phone them?' The men looked at the ground about a yard in front of their feet.

Flies buzzed around the body.

'They will want to question all of us,' Eddie said.

'Why all, Baas?'

'We have done nothing.'

'Yes, we have done nothing.'

'It was the woman. All have seen that.'

'But she must have . . . You must . . .' There was an explanation. They knew why she had stood beside the thorn bushes. They had fallen silent that morning when they passed her. They must know.

Suddenly Eddie remembered the baby. It must be somewhere on the kopie. The girl had not moved all day since taking up her position beside the thorn bushes. He had forgotten the baby.

'The baby, Altheus! Go and find the baby.'

'The baby, Baas?'

Rare anger flushed Eddie's face.

'Christ, man, go! Find the baby!'

As he said 'find the baby' he felt panic. He had forgotten the baby. In his obsession with the girl he had forgotten the baby. It must have been out on the kopie all day, yet he had not heard a cry. Altheus took half a dozen men and scrambled up the rocky slope. The rest of the men wandered off to the cook-boy's shed. Eddie went back to the office shack.

The girl was just as he had left her. He picked up the telephone, dialled and said he wanted to report a fatal accident. He pushed the stool towards the girl and pressed her down on to it. She did not protest but sat upright and calm. '. . . Lifted up her lovely head and . . .' Any moment he would have to hum out loud. It was the kind of thing people did in shock. There was a hip-flask in his briefcase. He poured a tot into the cap, offered it to the girl who ignored him, then tossed off the warm throat-scorching local spirit.

Altheus and the men were returning. When they reached the blanket, Altheus raised one corner and put down a small cloth-wrapped bundle.

'The baby?'

'Yes, Baas.'

'Dead?'

'Dead, Baas.'

'Has it been dead long?'

'Long, Baas.'

'Did she . . .? How did it die?' Altheus stared into Eddie's eyes for a few seconds, then looked along the track over the veldt. '. . . But last evening down in Lovers' Lane she strayed . . .' A few miles away the approaching police van raised a cloud of red dust. Altheus returned his gaze to Eddie and hunched his shoulders high.

'Who knows, Baas.'

THE NATIVE AIR

THE NATIVE AIR

I was nine when we went on that last picnic.

It was the time of year when swifts are having a last fling before settling down to raise their double broods, when the sun rises earlier than farm-labourers – and that's saying something – when cuckoos send their first indelible signals on Hampshire air. My family went on its last picnic.

My family. My family. Archards as old as the hills (perhaps going back to that Archard who was champion to Thomas, Earl of Warwick, who held his estates by payment of twelve broad arrows . . . then again, perhaps not). Radicals down the ages, arguing politics – even on picnics.

'Make the most of it.'

'It'll be over by Christmas.'

'Never.'

'See if you see if I an't right.'

'Like you was about Spain?'

Mothers and aunts have heard it all before.

'Must you keep on about it?'

Archards – good as They, probably better – leave their homes, which are all in the same small market-town, and gather in a flock of about twenty-five near Mountbatten's lodge gates.

'Battenburg!'

Grandfather never allows us to forget Their origins, never allows us to forget Queen Victoria, or who she married, and all her children. Who all the rest of That Lot married, and the Kaiser, and the Battenburgs.

Grandfather's a Republican, born and educated in a family with money. Now he's a blacksmith, an old Red. Somebody is always warning him.

'Thee's had better watch out, George. If we has this here war they'll shut up all old Bolshies like thee.'

My mother stops Uncle Harry with a look. She always does that when people start talking about Germany and war. I think we shall be bombed in trenches and gassed and I won't ever reach double figures next May. Please God, don't let us be bombed. Amen.

We leave the town on foot, pass the mill-race where we shall gather ritually in autumn to see salmon leap, take a cut across Green Hill and ramble along beside the River Test.

Even the littlest of us knows what 'going over Squab' means. An experience like no other, and the Archard family have been going over Squab summer after summer throughout time, taking our baskets and bags and bats and bottles, and memories of past picnics.

From Mountbatten's, Squab is about four miles, though such a walk can hardly be estimated in distance, better measured in time – perhaps time-standing-still. For us it is a distance of certain games, old jokes, feet in cow-pats and swills-off in the Test, a distance of mothers jumping at sudden bull bellows – it works every time.

'You blooming fool our Lennis! Frightening me like that.'

And fathers, used to working a fifty-hour week in the railway works, deposit a few of their years at each vaulted-over stile, to be collected on the homeward journey. It is a walk measured in excitement, fun and tightening family bonds.

We leave the open fields, over another stile and into the shadow of oaks. Into violets and primroses – or rhododendrons, or cowslips, billy-buttons, dog-roses or bitter green, bitter sharp hazels, or unripe blackberries – according to time of year. Up an incline where nature has never been able to compete with labourers' boots, and there is bare gravel.

The Butts. Halfway. The same notice is always here, always newly painted: 'WHEN THE RED FLAG SHOWS – BEWARE FIRING IN PROGRESS.'

> 'The People's Flag is deepest red
> It shrouded oft our martyred dead.'

Uncle Tom is the first proper Labour councillor in our town. Shop-steward for the Boilermakers, official of the Ancient Order of the Foresters, boy-scout captain, owner of the only camera in the family, hypochondriac, great believer in cascara sagrada for inner cleanliness and Imps for the chest. He knows only two songs, both about revolution; he sings them at parties, then puts his shoes on the wrong feet for a laugh – but only we know about that. A railwayman, the first elected working-class councillor in our town. He despises the fur-trimmed cloak and tasselled hat, but will wear it because people need to see we are as good as the other lot. When he was young he bought a revolver and was going to Russia, or was it Spain? He is my mother's brother, married to my father's sister. A second father to me.

> 'With heads uncovered swear we all
> To bear it onwards till we fall.'

Mothers and aunts raise their eyes to heaven.

'He's off again!'

'Our Tom – he don't change.'

'Can't take him nowhere!'

'They'll have him on the list too. Conchie.'

Uncle Harry's wrong, Uncle Tom will be one of the first to join the Local Defence Volunteers – you can't take him nowhere!

Up another slope and suddenly – always unexpectedly no matter how many times you've been before – a rough and saggy bit of chicken-wire fence, some sort of beaten pathway where rabbits have been, and stones disguised as tussocks lay in wait to stub our sandalled toes; suddenly – civilization! Well hardly that, yet somebody has touched the countryside, but not to disadvantage.

'We're here!'

'There's the swings.'

'We're here, we're here, we're here.'

At last we are over Squab. And over Squab lives Miss Biddlecombe.

Miss Biddlecombe. Fixed in our lives like Christmas and new socks at Easter. She had been married, but only for a day – not even the night. Miss Biddlecombe lives alone here in a clearing in Squab Wood. She grows every sort of fruit and vegetable, she keeps goats and pigs and assorted fowls.

Her home is a cottage – we call it that – it is roomy, probably ugly (but not to us), built of corrugated-iron and painted green. The door seems to be always open. Outside, the ground slopes gently into dense woods where rhododendrons grow in uncultivated grandeur.

Scattered about the clearing are benches, stools, old tree-stumps and assorted wavy-edged tables which have been left to the elements to distort, mellow and become so enlichened that they are as much part of the vegetation as when they were growing trees. There are gnarled and ancient medlars, quinces, costards, cherries and merries, and from their lower branches hang ropes for us to swing on.

'Beat you to the swing!'

'Not so fast.'

'Wait for me, wait for me.'

There is a general gallop of children. The older and more experienced among us get a head start because we have noticed the signs – the change from wildness to cultivation, saw the chicken-wire, knew we had arrived.

There is a general calling of mothers.

'Let the little ones have a chance.'

'Don't rush like that.'

'You big boys . . . careful!'

'Mind you don't fall!'

'Ah, leave'm be. They can't come to no real harm.'

We let the little ones have the swings and give them pushes. We prefer to swing by our hands from the branches – the boys in their short trousers swing by their feet, so we tuck our dresses into our knicker-legs not to be outdone. Mother says I shall break my neck.

The grown-ups have a discussion. It is important, we shall be here for hours, we have got first choice. Not that many people come here, but it is important.

'Where shall we go, then?'

'Here?'

'Bit near the house for the cricket.'

'Over there?'

'Be a bit shady when the sun goes down.'

'Want a bit of shade, though.'

'Make up your minds.'

'What about under the old crab tree?'

Ah, yes. Under him, like we did last year. Yes. Not too far to carry the trays, and you can keep an eye on the swings, and he's old now and not enough leaf to cut out the sun.

And before we get settled – how many teas?

'Well don't count the little ones.'

'Ah no – G.O.A.T.'S milk.'

'I like gee owe . . . that milk.'

'Ah, all right then, they might's well try it.'

So that's how many?

Mabe, Little Mabe and Auntie Mabe, Nella and Reg, Bertha and Nora and Father and you and me and . . . let's say three of the largest pots and plenty of milk. And who wants scones? And jam and cream? And fairy cakes and homemade-fresh-crusty-bread and buttercup butter which Miss Biddlecombe produces in her kitchen and honey from her straw hives?

'Something of everything and sort it out between us.'

'And fruit cake?'

'And seedy-cake?'

'We might's well, we don't come every day.'

'Might not be any much longer.'

'Oh, Father!'

'He's right . . .'

'Oh, Tom!'

'You can leave off that – we're over Squab.'

Uncles and fathers take care of the ordering. We sidle along with them.

'You children come away.'

'Miss Biddlecombe don't want you there.'

'Just you come on back here.'

Come away? Away from the mysteries of the dim interior of Miss Biddlecombe's kitchen?

'Might's well save your voice.'

'Might's well talk to yourself.'

'Ah, might's well.'

Might as well call pins from a magnet.

Miss Biddlecombe's kitchen draws my child's eyes and gradually the whole child until I stand by my father as he orders our teas. She is big and bosomy, in a long dress, a print apron and sensible shoes with little D's of fat like pin-cushions where the bar buttons across her large feet. Her cheeks are weathered red and her hair escapes from a rook's nest of a bun – just like my Nan who died.

She has heard us coming, she is pleased to see us again and greets us at the door with an uncomplicated smile for old friends – which we are. My father has been going over Squab since he was a boy and remembers the drama of her marriage of a few hours. Mother doesn't think he ought to talk about it but Father says it happened didn't it and there's no getting away from that. Dear Jesus, please don't let Miss Biddlecombe be sad. Amen.

'Well, Mr Archard. My dear Lord, goodness, how time do fly. And you girls, well I don't know! Proper little ladies now. It don't seem no more'n yesterday – and here we are again. What a winter it's been. That gale in March! You seen the old medlar I suppose? Blew down. He was a good old tree that one. Ah well, it comes to all of us. You won't want your tea yet a while. Say I have it ready . . .'

She looks above the trees judging the time – Uncle Ted says she's as good as the abbey clock –

'. . . in hour and a half? I got to go to the well, and I always does the big teapots for you don't I and I still got a pot of bramble jelly I was keeping for you but I got to get it down first, so it'll be a good hour and a half.'

Fathers and uncles turn away, sorry about the old medlar – they had scrumped him many a time for his strange fruits that were no good until they had decayed, then their juice dripped and left a strange perfume.

The cottage open door taunts and vamps. We hang about. On her wood fire a number of huge, black iron kettles steam, and what with them and the burning wood, and the sun on the iron walls, the smells and heat seem to boom out at us. We've known about respecting people's homes since before we could walk, but we would give anything to step inside.

'It's rude to stare into people's homes.'

'You ought to know better.'

'At your age!'

'Come on, Miss Biddlecombe got plenty to do.'

Mothers, busy at their leisure, unpack the fruit and sandwiches and hard-boiled eggs.

'We forgot the salt.'

'Ah, never mind, we can ask her for some with the tea.'

'I'll go.'

'We'll ask.'

'We'll go.'

It doesn't work, but it was worth a try.

Children in the upper age-range wander off to rediscover those places in the wood which are known only to those who have Archard blood. One or two cousins who were too young last summer, but are old enough this year, watch our every move. Nobody tells – watch and learn. Archards don't tell tales. Archards don't cry. Three of us are double-bond Archards. Special. A brother and sister married a sister and brother. Some Archards have red hair.

The new cousins are shown special moss that has scarlet lanterns, we pick some and try to make them stay in our eyebrows; shown nests, and spiders that look like brooches, shown the track where King William the Rufus – which means red hair – was carried dead, with an arrow in his chest and his blood dripping out all the way to

Winchester; told about peewits' eggs that you can sell for a pound each and are easy to find just lying up on Green Hill and we shall look for some on our way home; told the giggling secrets of lords and ladies and wild arum flowers being rude.

The boys pick up old acorn cups and stick them on their eyelids and noses, we make screeches with blades of grass and drum-beat hollow trees. Girls write boys' names on laurel-leaves and put them inside their vests next to their hearts, to work. The new cousins learn how we are bonded by sights and smells and sounds and textures.

The fathers polish a cricket ball on their only pair of flannels. They windmill their arms, strong from the daily use of heavy tools, the upper muscles have surprisingly fine white skin. They place their teenage fielders, who know from experience that they are unlikely to get much of a go at either bat or ball. Soon they will slope off and become kids again – just as their fathers are doing.

The younger children go off to the swings.

'Not where we can't see you.'

'No – not in the woods.'

'Next year, when you are big enough.'

. . . and the littlest ones stay with the mothers.

The mothers are doing what they do every day, a change though to be doing your job out of doors. There is not much letting down of hair, no equivalent to the cricket game, but it's company and Miss Biddlecombe is preparing some of the food.

Grandfather nods off for half an hour. It has been a long walk after a week at the forge shaping metal into railway engines.

We have found an animal skull, eaten clean and white. Eye-sockets. Teeth. Nose-holes. Teeth. Blood and fox and teeth like needles. Try to forget it.

'Ready. Coo-eee. Tea.'

It is Miss Biddlecombe.

Fathers down bats, leave the wicket and hurry to the pavilion for tea. The splintery table creaks as they put down the great brown teapots and water-jugs. Mothers sit and pour, and hand things out, and issue mind-outs, and carefuls and I didn't hear you say thank-yous. We know they like us to be a credit to them, so we try to be careful, but still drop our egg-yolks. We eat them gritty and try to remember our table-manners, and wonder why it is that everybody seems to have better sandwiches. I swap my neat triangles of Marmite for some hunks of bread and dripping.

Fathers sit on the grass, or benches, or tree-stumps as the fancy takes them. Children sit on the grass and no choice, wanting none. Grandfather never drinks anything but Instant Postum or beer. Here his beer comes flat and tepid. Grandfather takes things as they come – and lets us have a swig, secretly.

Teatime runs into rounders and piggy-in-the-middle – to give the little ones a chance. The last of the goat's-milk tea is drunk, the last jammy scone shared between two of the boys who have ever-open traps. The brown pots and thick cups are collected with enthusiasm by those of us who will try for another excuse to get into Miss Biddlecombe's kitchen.

How long have we been here? From early afternoon under full sun, to the first midge-rise from shady parts in the long grass. Shadows become purpled. Tomorrow's fine day is in a high-dancing cloud of gnats and mackerel in the sky. There must be days when the gnats are laid low and rooks make woolly baskets in the sky over Squab, but we shall not know of them.

'Everybody ready then?'

'You all packed up?'

'Got your cardigan?'

'Your football?'

'Your primroses?'

'Rhododendrons?'

'Bits of moss?'

'Animal skull?'

Are they serious? We haven't seen the big scene.

'Wait!'

'Please wait!'

'Oh, Dad, Dad.'

'We want to see her feed the birds.'

'Here she is.'

Her apron sags with the weight of the corn she carries.

'Chick, chick, here chick, chick.'

Hardly has she said 'chick' once, when there is a flapping, fluttering and squawking, hooting and honking from every part of the woodland. From everywhere come the birds. Geese, hens, cocks, ducks, drakes, guinea-fowl, pigeons and wigeons and all the woodland hangers-on. Goats, kids and a piglet or two run in. No, not at all like Disneyland. It is a sight like no other. Starlings locust-like over Birmingham, ostriches in huge flocks on the South African veldt, flamingos in pink thousands will never compete with her – feeding the birds over Squab.

The walk home is taken at the pace of the slowest. There is time to look, to listen to the zizz-zizz of the solitary bumble-bee and the on-and-on cuckoo and the fossilized eight o'clock curfew ribboning in the evening air. There is time for us to make wings from bracken and to stick the name of our sweethearts in burrs on our sleeves, make heads of rye-grass crawl up our arms, and to strip the ribs from plantain leaves to make tobacco secretly.

Mist rises from marshy ground. Mothers button up and frown at fathers who ought to know better than to dawdle once the sun has gone. Summer mists can be treacherous. Our mothers who were flappers dancing the charleston and the cakewalk ten years ago, have become old wives without intending to. They know that there's something nasty about a summer mist, and Aunt Rose will have to make her Barbados sugar and snail cure again if we hang about here.

At the bottom of Green Hill, where it has been for centuries, is the Horse and Jockey.

'Going in for a quick one?'

Ah . . . Grandfather could do with a pint . . . maybe four or five . . . back at the forge tomorrow.

'We ought to get on.'

'We got the greenhouse to shut.'

'The horse to see to.'

'The baby to see to.'

So, those who have no horses to water, pigs to feed or children too tired to take any more, go into the garden at the back of the Horse and Jockey to round off the perfect day with a glass of cold bitter. Those of us still young enough to appreciate it, get a glass of sharply-sweet, brilliant saffron-yellow draught lemonade. Our tongues will still be coloured in the morning.

As we walk home from the Jockey, the twilight runs out and the moon rises. We go to bed with a lick and a promise.

After the excitement of the day, my sister breathes her tiny night-time asthma wheeze close to my ear. Sometimes when I listen I think that she isn't really my sister but a field-mouse who has been enchanted and there will be a reward when she is returned to her real family of field-mice.

I can just see the picture of the lady in the crinoline with her stupid poem, 'Roses for remembrance,/Summer's sweetest flowers,/Yielding their sweet fragrance,/To bless the passing hours.' Usually I hate her for never doing anything except look at the blobs she says are roses, but not tonight. I am still full of whatever it is I get from my big family when we are all together.

The night is full of smells and sounds.

The hawthorn hedge that was cut this morning, the newly-turned earth of the front garden, the Seven Rubbing Oils on my sister's chest, next-door's lilac and the chips they are frying.

In the distance the late train to Bristol toots to Mr Hopkins in the signal-box. I've been there with Grandfather. It is like being inside a real toy, it smells of the hot stove and burning coke, tea and Brasso; messages are passed on in clicks and bells.

A whiff of Grandfather's Nosegay tobacco.

My mother is cutting the bread for the slices of lamb my father is carving, ready for work tomorrow.

Grandfather's boots crunch on the gravel as he goes to fasten the gate.

'Goodnight, George.'

'Ah, goodnight, Bert.'

That's Mr Nutland.

'Had a good day?'

That's Mrs Nutland.

'We saw you going off.'

'We've been over Squab.'

'It's been a nice day for it.' She walks on.

Mr Nutland will see Grandfather in the morning, on the train going to work, exchanging no more than a nod. He lingers.

'We haven't been over Squab for years.'

'It don't change.'

'Ah.'

'Seems further these days, though.'

'Might as well make the most of it while we can.'

'Ah, you're right there.'

'D'you reckon it'll come then?'

I listen hard, straining my ears, not wanting to hear. Grandfather knows everything about politics and economics and unions. If he says there will be a war, then there will be. Heavenly Father, please don't let there be a war. Amen.

'Good war's just what They want. Never did harm to profit. Shan't have no unemployed, Bert.'

'Ah.'

'They can always find money for a good war.'

'You're about right, George.'

'You won't see many of That Lot in the front line, though.'

'And that's a fact, George.'

'I give it till the end of the summer.'

I know now that there will be a war, and that I shall probably not reach double figures. All the time I've waited to be ten.

'Night then, George.'

'Night, Bert.'

Grandfather comes up the path quietly singing one of his party songs.

> 'Up the ladder with the bricks and mortar,
> Down the ladder with the empty hod,
> All we want are labourer's wages,
> We're the boys to carry them along.
> Oh!
> There's money in the country,

It's locked up in the store,
We fork it out most quickly
When we want to go to war,
The Rolling Trades, in motion,
We ask for nothing more
That seems to be the cry all over England.'

He comes indoors, places his working boots and blacksmith's spark-cap near the back door ready for six-thirty tomorrow morning and the railwayman's train. Before he leaves, he will have a pint of Instant Postum made with plenty of sugar, and a piece of fruit cake, or perhaps lardy-cake or doughnuts. One of the things I've been waiting to be grown up for is having cake for breakfast like him. He won't even have the lamb sandwiches Mother and Father have been making. Sweet tooth, he bends hot metal with Co-op jam or lemon curd.

The gaslamp in the street flickers and it occurs to me quite suddenly that God isn't true. I felt like this when I realized that there was no Santa Claus. Relieved, contained, glad it was all done by people who loved you. No mystery, no magic, just people.

It will be a long time before it will be safe to tell anyone – my school is C of E, and next year I'm going to be Confirmed.

The pipes bang as my mother fills the kettle.

The familiar sound of my father rattling a spoon around in the pickle-jar.

Grandfather takes a bottle of beer from under the stairs.

SISTERS – UNDER THE SKIN

SISTERS – UNDER THE SKIN

It was odd that we didn't hear the doorbell in the night. There's no doubt that Sara's friends tried to waken us, but none of us heard – not even the children whose room was across the hall. Possibly it was because I had been in hospital for a few days, which meant that routines had been disrupted and we were all making up for it. The fact remains, though, that during the night they had tried to waken us four or five times, but it wasn't until dawn that I heard the bell go.

The Zulu overseer of the cleaners, James, was waiting.

'M'em, the girl Sara. The other girls can do nothing. Can the M'em come?'

'Is she ill?'

'She is . . .' he searched the ground for the right word. 'She is unwell. Emily is with her.'

Of course, Emily would be. Emily was always in the midst of everything.

As I climbed the last step to the servants' living quarters on the roof, I heard her clearly above the hubbub.

Emily's massive bosom was the source of her command. She weighed twice that of the other women servants, and was as tall as any of the men. Nobody had such a magnificent sounding-board to enhance voice quality.

English, Xhausa, kitchen-Kaffir, she could out-boom everyone.

She saw me and detached herself from the crowd, shoving people to one side.

'Here she is. Here is the Medam. Medam, over here.'

She spread her arms wide and I ran the gauntlet of inquisitive Africans. Ill at ease, an intruder in their territory, I kept my head down and they made way for me.

Emily received me with ponderous gravity.

'The Medam is well again?'

'Oh, I wasn't ill – just a little operation.'

She nodded knowingly. 'In the woman hospital.'

I don't know how she knew, perhaps she didn't – an educated guess. Anyhow, that is where I had been for the past week.

'Things will be better for you now.'

'Yes. Thank you, Emily. Much better.'

She turned to a little group of women eating mealie-pap straight from little saucepans.

'I said the English Medam would come.'

Contempt for those who hadn't expected me to go up on the roof.

'I say to James he must tell the English Medam the Worm has come to the Girl.'

My stomach turned over. Oh God. Worms. That's what it was. You don't have to live in South Africa long before you learn an entirely new set of possible attacks upon the body. Don't swim in rivers. Wash everything that isn't cooked. Be careful about water-melons. Be careful about the spring milk. Wear the shoes, Medam, the jiggers will eat the toes! 'The Worm has come to the Girl.' I dreaded loathsome and unknown, disgusting infection.

It was one of those moments when an experience is so alien that it is difficult to relate to it. Yesterday I was behind huge plate-glass windows . . . polish, space, air-conditioning, in the luxurious surroundings of the private wing of the Rand Clinic. Today I was on the roof surrounded by black faces and lines of washing, little cooking-stoves, washing-troughs and rows of shed-like rooms and 'The Worm has come to the Girl'.

Emily turned to the little crowd which wanted to see what I would do.

'Go, go,' she waved her massive arms. 'This is not the carnival parade.'

The servants picked up their employers' washing or mops and brushes and drifted off to work. I was left standing with Emily and James.

'Wait here!' she ordered, and James hunkered down at her command and took out a flat, pinched-out dog-end and lit up. Emily beckoned and I followed.

'It is the Girl. The Worm has come to her in the night. Please sit.' She indicated a wooden stool which she brushed off with her apron.

'Shall I phone the doctor?'

She didn't answer, but turned to James and said, 'You hear, the Medam will phone a doctor?'

James grinned at me.

'Right then, show me which is her room and I'll go and see how she is. I can't get the doctor out until I know what's wrong.'

I was still standing. Again she dusted off the stool.

I sat.

'Does the Medam know what is the Worm?'

I shook my head.

'It is,' she lowered her voice confidentially and turned her head away from James, 'a thing that comes to many girls – very much when they come to This Place.'

'This Place' was the name Sara always used for

Johannesburg – the city, but I got the impression that Emily was referring to here, Chaucer Hall, the flats.

'It has come to your Girl.'

I assumed that she was trying not to talk indelicately to the young Madam.

'You mean?' I mimed holding myself as though suffering cramps.

'No, no, no.' She waved her hand back and forth erasing the idea. 'This Worm – it is . . . bad spirit.'

Bad spirit. When Sara spoke about bad spirit, I had taken it to mean feeling out of sorts, down, depressed. Some normally friendly woman passing along the corridor head down and withdrawn, would be 'full up of bad spirit today'.

'Well, where is she? I've come to see her.'

This was Emily at her most exasperating. In the corridor you could always break away from her with some excuse or other, but here she had me trapped.

Emily lowered her lids and shook her head.

'Medam, I will tell you. This thing, this Worm, it makes the girls not know what they do. Medam, did you not hear your Girl screaming?'

I caught glimpses of movement out of the corner of my eye. Several women were pretending to be busy, they were mostly women I knew well, from our own corridor. What was going on between me and Emily was evidently of intense interest.

'No, I didn't hear anything until James came.'

'Medam, we have come for you many times in the night.'

'I know, I know . . .'

She put up her broad hand, full of command. 'It is all right, Medam, you could not hear the doorbell, or even the knocker. Sara's bad spirit would not allow . . .'

I think it was my unease that brought me to my feet, but for some reason I kept my voice down. 'Emily, that's a lot of nonsense. If you don't show me where Sara is, I shall ask somebody else.'

'Very well, Medam.'

I followed her through the rows of washing almost to the edge of the building. It was very high up. The parapet was not much more than waist-high.

When Emily unlatched one of the doors I found that I had been holding my breath.

'Sara's room, Medam.' She held open the door for me and followed me in.

Coming from the brilliant morning sun, the tiny cell of a room appeared pitch-black.

'Switch on the light, Emily.'

There was the rattle and scrape of matches. I felt ridiculous, familiarly ridiculous, one of my 'why don't they eat cake?' kind of questions. There wouldn't be electricity up here, would there! Emily lit a candle then a kerosene lamp. The wick needed trimming, curly threads of lamp-black rose from the glass chimney. Marie Antoinette went to open a window. Idiot! This was up here! No windows!

Very quickly my eyes adjusted to the soft light. Emily was leaning over a bed.

'Sara! My girl! The Medam has come.'

There was no response. She prodded the mound of bedclothes.

'Sara! You must unwind. The Medam will not like you to spoil the blankets.' Then, as though we were discussing the merits of brand-names, she said to me, 'She is lucky you have bought for her American blankets, they do not stretch with winding.'

The mound on the bed was wound mummy-like in the pink blankets we had recently taken a morning to choose, and covered with a bright 'native' blanket; two hands clutching the hem of the top blanket was all of Sara that was visible.

'Sara. It's me. Aren't you well?' Sara made a small sound.

'Unwind yourself, my girl.' Emily's voice was deep and beautiful but her tone was unpersuasive.

'Shh.'

Emily took a step back, perhaps offended . . . ah well, I would apologize later.

'Sara. I'm going to get Dr Wunch to come. But I'll have to tell him what's wrong.'

Her fingers moved, unlocking from the blanket.

'Give me a hand.'

Gradually, like unbandaging a tender injury, Emily and I freed Sara from her cocoon of pink blankets. I was shocked at the sight of her.

No children were allowed to visit at the clinic, but every day during my stay there, Sara had wheeled the push-chair and brought my children to where they could wave to me. She had beamed and waved too, and had smoothed the boys' hair and straightened their collars, indicating to me that I needn't worry, they were being taken care of. She always washed her glasses and brushed her teeth several times a day and they glittered up at me – she had been her usual self.

Sara was one of those people who when not wearing their glasses appear to be missing a feature. But it wasn't just the absence of glasses that made her appear strange. Her face had lost its brown shine and was a sickly yellow and appeared to have a dusting of dry grey.

'I am sorry.' Her voice was thin, weak, like a very old person, she sounded exhausted.

'It's all right, I'm going to call Dr Wunch.'

Emily rustled her starched apron.

'You see, my girl, how lucky you are.'

I wished Emily wouldn't do it, it was always so embarrassing. It wasn't obsequiousness, but I think she felt she must take it upon herself to mention certain things, in case I should think Sara didn't appear grateful enough for such luck as pink blankets and Medams who asked doctors to call.

'Emily, would you take a message down to the flat?'

'I shall ask the Baas?'

'Say that Sara needs a doctor. If he wants to know what's wrong, just say . . . it's fatigue . . . say she is overtired.' Obviously Emily preferred 'fatigue', I heard her telling David:

'That girl has got fatigue. The Medam is sending for the doctor.'

After Emily left there seemed to be a vacuum in the little room, a surprising chill, and I felt uneasy. I sat on the edge of the bed. Not only was it the first time I had been in Sara's room, it was the first time that I had ever seen her prone. In the kitchen she perched on a high stool, on the balcony no amount of persuasion would make her use a deck-chair, choosing to sit as she did on picnics, on the ground with her legs under her and her skirts tucked decorously round them. Seeing her in bed was like the unique occasion when my father took to his bed after an accident at work.The centre-pole from which hung the tent of my life was no longer upright. I hadn't realized how very much I depended upon her.

'Sara?'

She opened her eyes. She was crying. Not good, normal tears, but a constant heavy stream that ran from the outer corner of her eyes. I didn't know what to say. She was a stickler for protocol. It was she who had made the rules by which we lived. We had wanted her to live au pair, but she made few concessions. At the beginning I tried getting her to at least call us Mr and Mrs instead of the awful Medam and Masta. She called the children by their first names which at least was better than old Daniel, who cleaned the cooker, who used Master, Little Master and Very Little Master. She liked her uniform, and would eat only in the kitchen. I felt sure that she would disapprove of me sitting on her bed.

It suddenly occurred to me that I had sent for our own doctor, and I had no idea how the system worked under apartheid. Did white doctors treat blacks? Surely they must, there were very few black or coloured doctors. And Dr Wunch practised in the salubrious suburbs, how would he react to being called out to a black girl in a servant's room? Emily hadn't seemed surprised. Perhaps it would be all right. I would have to just wait and see what happened.

'Is there anything I can get you? Would you like some tea?'

'Emily will make it.'

Three times she had spoken, each time she had omitted the 'Medam' with which she usually prefaced everything she said to me. Maybe it took something like this to break down the barrier between us. God knows we needed each other. Each of us days of travelling from our homes. Each of us living by chance in an alien place, and longing to be in our own country. Living under the same roof, dusting the same furniture, sharing the same children. My roof, my furniture, my children . . . perhaps her dignity was saved by the protocol.

I heard Emily's voice and went to the door.

'The Baas says OK, he has talk to the doctor. He will come. I tell the Baas it is all right for him to go to his office. I will see to every thing.'

Sara would hate having Emily in her kitchen, but I said how nice it was of her and asked her to go down and make some tea for us. She went, telling everybody that she was going to make tea in the English Medam's flat.

What would Emily have been under different circumstances? She needed to be expansive, organizing, involved with people, she should have been in charge of some large institution instead of serving a single woman who was away from home most of the day.

Back in the little room I noticed a low stool which I placed beside Sara's bed and sat down.

'Emily's gone to get some tea, and the doctor will come later.' She nodded acknowledgement.

'Sara, have you been ill like this before?'

'Yes, sometimes. Not since I have come to the flat.'

'Have you had treatment before?'

'Yes, they are doing research.'

'Research?'

She didn't say anything for a minute, then she filled her lungs and let out an enormous sigh. Her body seemed to relax and sink into the bed. A bit of her more normal colour appeared in her face.

'At the hospital. On Thursdays.'

Thursdays.

Ever since she had lived with us she had gone to stay with her friends in Soweto at weekends, and Thursday afternoons she took the bus into the city. I had always assumed she went wandering round the stores.

'Do you want to talk about it? Do you know what is wrong? Have you got anything to take?'

Before she could answer, Emily rattled in with our best tray beautifully laid up. Fine china teapot, sugar-bowl, jug, basin, one cup and saucer and two thick kitchen mugs. The council-house child still feeling guilt.

Damn you, Emily!

No, no. Fool. It wasn't anything to do with Emily. She was behaving like the well-trained servant that she was. She didn't make the rules, they were made by people like me. Them and us, black and white rules. As usual I tried to apologize for my thoughts with an action. I handed her the cup and saucer and Sara and I had mugs. She didn't stop long, saying that she had better get back down as she had two flats to look after.

I sweetened Sara's tea with three spoonfuls of sugar as she liked it, and she accepted a biscuit.

'That's better,' I said.

She pulled herself up in the bed and patted her hair. Slowly, the Sara I knew began to emerge. I gave her her glasses and before putting them on she polished them on the bedcover.

'Medam, the hospital. Before I came with you I was ill a lot of times. It was the Worm. Has Emily told you?'

'She called it that, but I don't know what it is.'

She gave me her wise look.

'You do know. You also have worm pills. The pills I get from the drug store for you? The yellow ones?'

Of course!

'In England, we say it is the black dog,' I said.

'What does it do?'

'It leaps on our back. You've seen me with the black dog on my back.'

'In Swaziland, we say it is the Worm that comes in the night.'

'How long . . . ?'

'First time when I was in Cape Town. It came from nowhere. I was frightened. Another girl gave me something to smoke, but it made me crazy. It came again some times, then I got used to Cape Town, I had a boyfriend.

He went over the border and I did not see him again.'

Why couldn't I simply hug her? It was what we both needed, but the barrier between us she had erected for her own protection. She had to live up here. She was an itinerant worker allowed to exist here only because she owned a Passbook. I should have taken a chance and put my arms round her, but we were too much alike. We were each encased in the shells we had made to protect ourselves from rejection.

Emily would have done it.

'Do they call it the Worm at the hospital?'

'Yes.'

'Why?'

'It is a worm that eats at the heart.'

I thought that she was going to cry again, but she stopped the tears by hard polishing of her glasses.

'Do you think the pills are any good?' she asked.

'No, do you?'

'I think they feed the Worm.'

'Was it too much for you looking after the children while I was at the clinic?'

'No, no. I am better now I live with children again. We had plenty of fun.' She smiled. 'Can I ask you about it? Your black dog.'

'What is there to ask? It is no different.'

'That is what I wanted to know, if it was the same.'

'Only that we call it depression.'

'That is the proper name for the Worm. At the hospital the doctors are trying things on many girls who have this, they say it is maybe anxiety that is the cause. We must leave our children. We lose our sisters and brothers, our mothers are at home, we worry. They say it is more common than any other illness for girls.'

'And are they all given the same pills?'

'Some have two milligram, some have five milligram. They try us on different sorts, some only at night, some three times in a day. These are mine, Medam.'

Her cardboard pill-box was under her pillow. Except for the name on the label it was identical to the one in my medicine chest. Same box. Same label. Same contents. Same instructions.

'Valium. 5mg. One tablet to be taken three times a day.'

Food for the Worm. Tit-bits for the Black Dog. Twilight for the sisterhood.

WILLOW-HERB AND SPEEDWELL

WILLOW-HERB AND SPEEDWELL

Rick, swinging the picnic basket, was out of earshot. Ella, imagining herself in various situations, spoke aloud, trying it out.

'Same age as Sophia Loren . . . A bit younger than Jackie Onassis!'

Smiling. 'Well, actually I'm fifty – it sounds a hundred doesn't it?'

God! It did sound a hundred.

She raised her voice.

'Fifty, Rick. Sounds a lot older than forty-nine.'

He wasn't listening but nodded all the same. It didn't matter much, they'd had plenty of not-listening conversations in thirty years of marriage. He would talk about hardware and software, bytes and megabytes and she would nod. She would tell him about Elisabeth Frink's sculpture or Sylvia Plath's poetry. Each knowing and giving the necessary response – they *had* lived together for thirty years.

'There's a lot more old-man's-beard, Rick,' she called. 'The wayfarer trees have grown too. Can't see the valley any more.'

Rick had stopped beside a five-bar gate.

'It's ten years. Things grow in ten years,' he said.

His arm spread wide, he indicated the gate, presenting it with a pleased smile.

'Look, they put the gate back. That'll keep the bloody cars out!'

It had been the bloody cars that had finally stopped them coming here.

They had discovered the place over twenty years ago. The boys had been babies and the gate had still been in good repair. Coming from the city, it had seemed like going into the wilderness. So high up on the Hampshire downs that you could sometimes see all the adjoining counties; a place where Ella and Rick could stretch out under the porcelain bowl of sky and let the kids roll down slopes and make caves in long grass – away from it all for a few hours.

It had been up here that she had first rebelled against domesticity – in thought only. Twenty years ago. Before the idea of the sixties got under way, before assertiveness, before feminism escaped from the intellectuals and women with money. 'Why should it bloody always be bloody me?' Simple thought, but take Marx for instance, he must have started with just a simple thought. Why?

All that she had said that time was, 'I'm going for a walk Rick, I'll leave you to put out the food.'

'It can wait. I shall only mess it up.'

And as always she had ended up feeling guilty. Rick was in the rat-race, men had enough to do without being bothered with domesticity. Women with modern houses and only a couple of kids, and washing-machines and hoovers and all day to do it in. Up and coming Young Exec. needed the weekends to relax. The rebellion was quelled.

Summers came and went. The babies became the kids, then the kids became the boys, and stopped making grass caves. They grew their way through kites and balsa-wood airplanes, flint arrow-heads and boredom. Ella and Rick had been drawn into the Young-Exec.-Estate-House-PTA circle and the picnics had become jolly expeditions. Other muesli-eating, squash-playing, state-educating parents who were up in things like the effect of lead and religion on children, came in company hatch-backs, picnicking from wicker baskets and wine-coolers. They had all laughed a lot about their ragged-ass beginnings and their present upward mobility, talked socialism and put up as Labour in council elections. Stripped-pine Marxists.

One day the gate-latch disappeared, next the spring-hinge was ripped off so that the gate could be propped open, and so the bloody cars had started to come. At first just one or two families bumped up the flinty path, and parked under the beeches so that they hadn't got to walk at all. Then, one summer the whole gate had been thrown in the hedge, and it seemed as though half Hampshire discovered Beacon Hill. Cars parked all round the summit as close as in a city carpark. People unloaded their belongings beside their bumpers and sat close to their cars. Transistor radios squeaked cricket commentary and quacked music.

'Why can't they just enjoy it?' Ella said, waving her arm at the field-patterns, the beeches and encircling horizons.

'They do!' Tom, eleven, had a knack of drawing Ella back from the brink of talking like a company wife.

Fifty!

Reached your half-century, Ella's mother would have said. Now you're in double figures; when Ella was ten. Into your teens. Out of your teens. Best years of your life. Fair, fat and forty! Menopausal years. Over the hill. Mother had euphemisms for age, birth, cancer, death. Now Mother was dead – passed over. Nobody now to tell Ella to buckle down to it in a marriage.

Ella had buckled down all right. Worked in a typing pool to save for the first house deposit, then seven shirts a week for the Young Exec., hundreds of four-hourly feeds, a million dirty nappies. Taught socially acceptable table-manners, eased frightened or stubborn children into the school system. Dutifully buckling down. Drifting. Waiting for Rick to get to the top. Waiting for the boys to go to school, waiting for them to finish their 'O'-levels, 'A'-levels, university, apprenticeships. Waiting uselessly for her mother's speech to return after the stroke.

And now – fifty!

'Come on.'

Rick held open the small side-gate. It was one of the things she liked about him, a down-to-earth kind of courtesy that stemmed from his working-class origins, quite unlike the correct mannerliness of some of his present colleagues who bobbed up and down when their wives came into a room but left them to lug the shopping home.

Through the gate the path widened and soon they were on the crest. They exchanged pleased looks. The white obelisk was as it had been twenty years before, barely visible amid long, seeding grasses. Far below in the growing heat-haze barns glinted, grazing land looked like bowling-greens and cattle seemed not to be moving. No matter where they let their gaze fall, they could see no other human being. The simple act of replacing the old gate with a substantial one with a padlock and a small separate access, had defeated the bloody cars. Beacon Hill had been returned to the few people who were prepared to walk the mile or so of track.

'Shall I put the food out?' Rick asked.

'If you like. I don't want anything yet.'

Rick put the basket in the shade. It contained hardly anything compared with those she used to pack when the boys were growing up – just a couple of peaches, grainy bread, some cheese and a bottle of wine. The stuff they used to hump up here! Rick had once bought an expensive basket from Harrods, all fitted out with cups and saucers, knives and forks, boxes and flasks. Posh, and it weighed a ton. Today, everything they needed was contained in a small shopping basket.

Rick spread the blanket and stretched out on his back; after a look at the Sport and Business sections of the *Observer*, he would doze. Ella wandered off down the slope. This was the moment. Anticipation. Elation. Even when they had come with the crowd, she had nearly always managed to go off on her own. There had once been a clever discussion between two of the crowd who were English teachers, as to whether Ella was Eustacia Vye or Tess Durbeyfield and she had wished that Rick had understood what they meant.

This was where she felt at ease. The clutter of loyalty, responsibility, guilt and love that surrounded her thinking, dissolved into the haze that hovered a few feet above the chalk-hill flowers. She sometimes thought of herself as living in a cocoon like that of a caddis-fly larva, except that, instead of the camouflage being detritus of the river-bed, hers was stuck over with bits of wife, mother, neighbour, magistrate, committee-member.

Here she emerged and was on a par with yellow butterflies, blue scabious and junipers. She took out a small pad and a couple of pencils.

Fifty years is a hell of a long time. Still pretty, though. True, a bit of a chin, and the underside of the arm shows that the supply of hormones is lessening. Men still look twice – mature men, men like Rick. Tom had been four, and now he's twenty-five, married, living on an estate, a Young Exec. – they call them Admins. these days. Andy on a year's VSO before going back to try again for a qualification. Rick settled in an office with two phones, lined curtains and Wilton carpeting.

The July sun was almost overhead. Heat flowed over the hill like a tide, drawing out the smell of earth and grass and chalk-hill flowers. The air was still and full of insect sound and the valley quivered in the haze. Ella lay down and put her hands behind her head as she had done that other time staring into the blue bowl.

She could go back to Rick right now. Come straight to the point. Rick, I know it will create havoc, it will mean you learning to use the cooker, push a trolley round the supermarket and do some of the housework . . . No, that would sound aggressive. 'Assertiveness is . . .' She couldn't remember, it had to do with being aware of one's own basic . . . rights? Yes, and with respect for yourself and using the right approach. Rick, I think I would like to read for a degree in Art History. Rick, I've been up to the Art College and . . . Rick, do you know what I've always wanted . . . ?

Rick, I want . . . I want . . . I want . . .

The words seemed to hover. From the blue bowl, the solid hill, the quivering heat-haze, came the sharp-tongued retort, 'Well, Andrew, we can't have everything we want can we?' Ella's own shrill voice, irritable at the small child's wants. 'Well, we can't have everything we want.' Andy's hurt look, Ella's guilt. What had he wanted that had made her so shrill? She had done a lot of that at one time. Sharp. Snapping. Resentful. Guilt. Remorse. Always the guilt. She put her arms round his knees to draw him down to her. He was stiff, unyielding, punishing her, then allowing himself to sink into her lap – generous forgiveness.

She had picked a clear-blue creeping flower.

'See? It's called speedwell. Look how little it is, and you see the big tall flowers . . .' she had reached out to some rose-bay willow-herb, tall and slender, '. . . it's not a bit of good the speedwell saying I want, I want, I want to be a tall pink flower. It can't be and there's nothing it can do about it, so it might just as well be pleased that it's blue and beautiful, and glad that the bees like it just as much as they like the pink one.'

'Don't it be cross sometimes?'

'It certainly be very cross sometimes.'

Ella kissed the baby who was now trying to show solidarity with the starving millions in Africa, and her cheeks were wet. Why do we have to practise being parents on our own kids? She had tried to do it right.

God! It was all a hundred years ago, wasn't it.

Read for a degree. What was that compared to bringing up your kids? What a hash she'd made of it, though. Women did, she had learned that much, learned it too late to be of much use. The terrible early years looking into other prams. Trying to keep everything the same as before there were any babies. Never enough hours, enough sleep, enough money, enough understanding.

The trouble was you didn't know you were making a hash of it. With most things you can tell, but with your kids you don't know until the damage is done. Maybe that's why the grass always seems greener on the men's side of the fence – seemed greener. Men like Rick, anyhow. Make a hash of an interview and you didn't get the job. Make a hash of the job and you didn't get promotion. Make a hash of your finals and you didn't get your degree. The results were immediate. Rectifiable.

Make a hash of your kids and . . .

She must have been lying there a long time. The

direction of the sun had changed and was now reflecting off some shiny surfaces way across the valley. Two box-kites hung in the air there. That's where the bloody cars must go now they couldn't get up here. She turned and saw Rick unpacking their lunch. She would go back and resume her undemanding life as the wife of a company director and be satisfied. What she had said to Andy was true, you can't have everything.

Face the fact that there were things you could never have, never be. Face the fact and contain the frustration, the resentment. You could tell pretty whimsical little tales to three-year-olds, who couldn't detect a false analogy. The speedwell has no capacity for frustration or resentment.

Slowly, Ella wandered back to where Rick was pouring the wine. If he said 'A penny for them?' it would mean that he had noticed that she had been crying and was giving her a chance to talk if she wanted. He would think that she had been remembering other picnics when they came with the crowd. How would he react if she answered, 'I've been crying for the future.' He would look non-plussed. Ella in one of her dramatic moods – arty, what with her poetry, and her painting.

Taking the glass he held out for her she sat beside him looking out over the valley.

'A penny for them?'

His hand took a familiar route down her back.

'They're worth more than that.'

Next he would caress her shoulders.

Playing the same game they had played the first time she went out with him. She held out her hand and he gave her a coin, he saw too late that it was a one-pound coin. He wrestled for it. Lost.

'They had better be worth it.'

He caressed the bare brown skin of her shoulders.

'I've been a speedwell too long, I want to be a rose-bay willow-herb.'

He used to get irritable when she said things like that, or when they had been to an art exhibition with some of the crowd, putting her down, making her feel silly.

'Oh yes? Nice. Not worth a quid.'

His hand was moving down her back again.

'You're still a good lay, El.'

On the whole, it was better up here now than it had been years before. Going home didn't matter, wasn't a thing to be dreaded at the end of the day. Rick wasn't competing any longer. No kids, no mortgage, no need for keeping up appearances. All that insecurity – gone. And if she had made a hash of bringing up the kids, it was too late to do anything, and anyway they seemed to have turned out much like other kids . . . better than many.

She would soon get used to being fifty as she had forty or any of the old milestones. And she was still Rick's good lay. Some of the old crowd had tried out swapping and temporary arrangements of one sort or another. She didn't think Rick had ever been involved, but during the sixties . . . ah, it didn't matter, none of its mattered. Rick's lay. That had always been pretty good.

His hand on her shoulder was now still, only the thumb making circles in the hollow at the base of her skull. The two box-kites drifted, and reached a point where she saw them balanced, framed in her mind's eye. She took up her pencils and sketch pad.

Rick picked up the sports pages again. 'I reckon it's time you did that seriously, you aren't getting any younger.'

'What is it, then, do you fancy laying an art student?'